PANTERA SECURITY
LEAGUE
COLLECTION 1

ALEXANDRA IVY
& LAURA WRIGHT

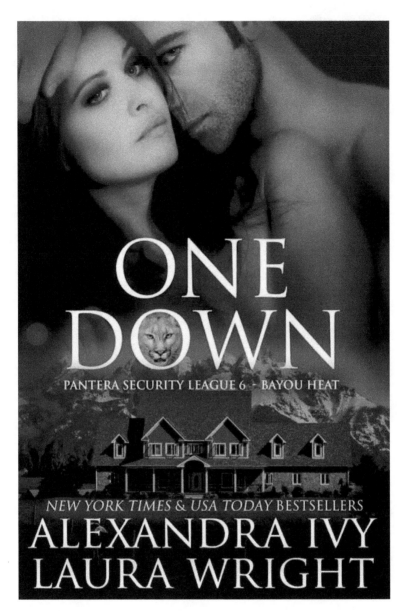

ONE
DOWN

PANTERA SECURITY LEAGUE 6 - BAYOU HEAT

NEW YORK TIMES & *USA TODAY* BESTSELLERS
ALEXANDRA IVY
LAURA WRIGHT

ONE DOWN
PANTERA SECURITY LEAGUE 6 - BAYOU HEAT

ALEXANDRA IVY
LAURA WRIGHT

From the Authors

While writing the Bayou Heat series, the two of us have often discussed fun, side adventures that wouldn't exactly fit into the overall storyline of the books. Eventually those ideas could no longer be denied and we started chatting about a separate "Six" characters who were all living outside the Wildlands. Breaking with each of their born-to factions, these Pantera are the baddest of the bad, and willing to work in that gray area between right and wrong. In other words, they're special ops warriors who are willing to do whatever necessary to protect their people. And so the Pantera Security League was born.

Unfortunately, we're both overwhelmed with deadlines which meant that it might be years before we could actually write the books, so the solution was to try something completely new. We would write the same story together, each taking turns to layer in the action, emotion, and suspense that readers expect in a Bayou Heat story.

We hope you enjoy the stories! We certainly love writing them!

Happy Reading,
Alex and Laura

Legend of the Pantera

To most people, the Pantera, a mystical race of puma shifters who live in the depths of the Louisiana swamps, have become little more than a legend.

It was rumored that in the ancient past twin sisters, born of magic, created a sacred land and claimed it as their own. From that land came creatures who were neither human or animal, but a mixture of the two.

They became faster and stronger than normal humans. Their senses were hyper-acute. And when surrounded by the magic of the Wildlands they were capable of shifting into pumas.

It was also whispered that they possessed other gifts— telepathy, witchcraft, immortality and the ability to produce a musk that could enthrall mere mortals.

Mothers warned young girls never to roam alone near the swamps, convinced that they would be snatched by the Pantera, while young men were trained to avoid hunting anywhere near the protected Wildlands.

Not that the warnings were always successful.

What girl didn't dream of being seduced by a gorgeous, mysterious stranger? And what young man didn't want to try his skill against the most lethal of predators?

As the years passed, however, sightings of the Pantera became so rare that the rumors faded to myth.

Most believed the species never existed at all.

All except a group of humans led by Christopher Benson, the CEO of Benson Enterprises. The reclusive, mysterious businessman has made a fortune by capturing Pantera and experimenting on them in his secret laboratories. He's created serums with their blood that can offer youth and vitality to his rich friends. And injected warriors with Pantera DNA in an attempt to create super soldiers.

But his ultimate endgame for the Pantera is only now being revealed.

Can they discover the truth of his evil scheme before it's too late?

CHAPTER 1

The golden puma slowed his pace, sliding through the purple shadows at the edge of the Wildlands, nostrils flared, breathing heavily. The large, lethally dangerous animal moved with the liquid grace of a predator, his eyes cat-gold and his massive paws barely making a mark on the mossy ground. He'd arrived early to score a long run in his cat form just inside the border of the bayou, enjoy a dose of the magic that allowed his kind to shift from human to puma. It was a pleasure he was rarely afforded.

After all, dead Pantera couldn't return home, could they?

Scare the shit out of the family who'd already mourned them.

Cerviel's puma sneered. Such were the lives of The Six.

As an invisible part of the Diplomatic faction of the Pantera, he'd devoted the past several months to trying to infiltrate Christopher Benson's vast business empire. He'd fiercely hoped for an opportunity to kill the bastard. He had the go-ahead. Unfortunately, the human male who'd been responsible for capturing Pantera and using them as lab rats in his sick experimentations had apparently gone into hiding. The real subterranean kind. Like, down with the worms and the moles. Pretty much where he belonged.

Where Cerviel would love to put him permanently.

But no one, not even his own people—or the two pieces-of-shit Pantera who had been accused of aiding him—had a clue where Benson was hiding.

That didn't mean Cerviel hadn't been pissed when he'd received Raphael's text ordering him to return to the Wildlands. It was shit timing. He'd been deep undercover in New Orleans, earning the trust of several stockholders who had invested in Benson Enterprises. He was certain that with just a few more days he could've managed to find, coerce and/or threaten someone who could tell him where to locate Christopher.

Instead he'd jumped in his car and driven at the speed of light to discover why Raphael needed him. It wasn't just because he was a loyal Pantera. It was because he was a part of The Six: the ghost warriors of the Pantera Security League. A group of specialized fighters who took on the top-secret jobs the various faction leaders needed handled with utmost discretion. It was a kick-ass gig, and Cerviel loved it. But it sure as shit came with some complicated drawbacks.

Ceasing to exist being one of them.

A shimmer of power suddenly glistened around him, and when Cerviel glanced up he spotted the approaching puma he'd been waiting for. A huge, caramel-colored beast who was lethal as fuck. In seconds, the animal shifted into a tall male with equally golden hair and jade eyes that glowed with the sharp heat of his inner cat.

Raphael, the current head honcho of the Suits—Cerviel's born-to faction—and all-around badass.

Shifting quickly, and dressed in the custom Armani suit he'd been wearing when he'd hightailed it out of New Orleans a few hours ago, Cerviel stalked toward the male. Though slightly taller than Raphael, Cerviel was the leader's opposite in looks. Lean-muscled with bronzed skin and dark eyes, he wore his thick black hair to his shoulders. His features were finely chiseled and he currently sported a neatly trimmed goatee. It was no secret he preferred cunning to brute strength.

Ironman to The Hulk.

"You flashed the bat signal?" he drawled.

Raphael arched a brow. "Bat signal?"

Cerviel gave a lift of his shoulder. "You know Batman and the bat signal?" His leader's face remained set in grim lines. Clearly the older male's mood was as pissy as Cerviel's, or he thought superheroes were bullshit. "Never mind, you're more of a Fortress of Silence sort of dude," he muttered. "Why did you want me to meet you here?"

Raphael glanced around cautiously. There was nothing to see beyond the thick cypress trees and the tangled grass that was nearly waist-high in this area of the bayou. Still, the older male leaned closer, keeping his voice pitched low.

"I have a new assignment for you."

"Now?" Cerviel scowled. "I just managed to infiltrate Benson's boardroom. It's only a matter of time before I discover where the bastard's hiding and put a bullet in his brain."

"You can return to New Orleans after you're done with this," Raphael said, shoving a piece of paper in Cerviel's hand.

Cerviel glanced down, reading the brief note out loud. "*Code red. Dispose of all test subjects at Rattlesnake Ranch, China House, The Orchard, Mulberry Lane, Battle Creek, and RR.*" He lifted his head, glancing at his companion with a baffled gaze. "Is this supposed to make some sort sense?"

"Xavier intercepted the message while he was monitoring Benson's private cellphone," Raphael explained. "It's the only contact the sneaky piece of shit made since he went into hiding, so we assume it must be important enough for him to risk having his current position exposed."

Cerviel reread the note. The names sounded like a list of low-budget flicks.

"What do you want from me?" he asked.

"I used my contacts with the human IRS to trace a Rattlesnake Ranch in Wyoming to a man named Rick Donaldson," Raphael said.

Cerviel felt a stir of recognition. "Why is that name familiar?"

"He's a retired congressman."

The younger Pantera grimaced. Of course. A politician. Rattlesnake Ranch sounded like the perfect place for him.

"Any connection to Benson Enterprises?" he asked.

Raphael nodded, his eyes glowing with the golden power of his cat. "Donaldson was the one who pushed the military to offer several highly profitable contracts to Benson."

"Okay." Cerviel resisted the urge to yawn. "So we know that there's a politician named Donaldson in Wyoming who helped Benson peddle his weapons to the DOD," he said. "And?"

"And we believe the test subjects are Pantera," Raphael said. "Or humans that have been infused with our blood."

"You can't be certain," Cerviel said. He'd only been hunting Christopher Benson for a few months, but he'd discovered in that short amount of time that the ruthless man had his fingers in a lot of nasty pies. "Benson Enterprises' Frankenstein laboratories are an equal opportunity torture chamber. Not all of the prisoners have something to do with the Pantera."

Raphael shrugged. "Xavier did a little more digging.

Cerviel rolled his eyes. Xavier, the leader of the Geeks, was a brilliant computer whiz who'd ensured that the Pantera were not only on the cutting edge of technology, but that they had an electronic hacking system that would rival Homeland Security.

"Of course he did," Cerviel drawled.

As usual, Raphael ignored Cerviel's wry humor. The older male had two moods: grim and grimmer.

At least when he was working.

When it came to his mate and new daughter…well, the leader was a different male altogether.

"He ran across a message from Donaldson to Benson that assured him the 'animal' was in good shape despite the fact that one of Benson's friends had seen her and she'd recently been beaten."

Cerviel sucked in a sharp breath. They were all struggling to come to terms with the knowledge that their people had been being secretly kidnapped by Benson operatives and treated as lab rats. And worse, that several females had been used in ways that made his inner cat snarl in fury.

"Bastard," he breathed.

Raphael snorted. "You won't get an argument from me."

"You think she's the test subject?"

Raphael gave a lift of his hands. "That's the theory."

Cerviel frowned, not entirely sure where this was all going.

"What do you want from me?"

"I need you to travel to Wyoming and retrieve her before she can be disposed of."

Cerviel's frown deepened. Was the male serious? A single rescue? It was like going back to training, for fuck's sake.

"That's it? An asset retrieval?"

A faint smile curved Raphael's lips. "I knew it was more than your pretty face that made me choose you to be a part of the league."

Cerviel calmly flipped him off. "Why me? This is a job for one of the Hunters." He caught himself sneering. "Unless I'm to take out the congressman and a few of his friends before the snatch and grab, I don't understand—"

"We believe she's...special."

"Special?"

Raphael nodded. "After we intercepted the messages, I decided to do my own investigating."

"I don't understand."

A wicked smile curved Raphael's lips. "I managed to capture one of Benson's top lieutenants," he revealed. "After a few hours of questioning he admitted that no one but Benson knew anything about the 'test subjects' and that he was frantic to make sure they didn't end up in our hands."

Hmm. Cerviel studied his friend and leader. "How do you know he wasn't lying?"

Raphael looked cagey. "Trust me, we have a special lie detector."

Cerviel didn't demand an explanation. They'd learned that the humans who'd been infected with Pantera blood had all sorts of new, unexpected talents. He wouldn't doubt that one of them was a walking, talking lie detector.

Anyway, if it was a secret, Raphael wasn't going to share the intel no matter how hard Cerviel might press. It was Raphael's ability to keep his mouth shut that ensured no one but a handful of Pantera knew about "The Six."

"And if you can't reach her in the time allotted—"

Cerviel interrupted his superior with a dismissive, arrogant snort.

"If you can't reach her," Raphael repeated, his mouth suddenly tight and grim, his eyes flashing with a grave warning, "burn the place to the ground."

Cerviel raised one eyebrow. *Now this is interesting.*

"No one," Raph continued, a snarl threading his tone, "and I mean no one, can be allowed to leave the property with intel that could be dangerous to the Pantera."

"Dangerous? Or deadly?" When Raphael didn't answer, Cerviel gave him an understanding grin. No, he mused, this wasn't work for a Hunter—or any civilian member of the Pantera. "Talk to me about the ranch."

Raphael inhaled sharply. "It's located in the Star Valley," he said. "Over a thousand acres of prime real estate with a house the size of a football field."

Cerviel snorted. "Cozy."

"I'll text you the exact coordinates."

"Do you have an entry and extrication plan in place?"

"You'll fly to a private airfield. From there a chopper will drop you just outside the hot zone." Raphael glanced around as the wind rustled through the tangled grass. It was a reminder to both men that the dawn was swiftly approaching. "We're alone."

"Never can be too sure," Cerviel said dryly. "Don't want anyone seeing me. Ghost stories don't go down well around here."

Raphael nodded.

Asshole. "You going to make me ask?"

Raphael knew exactly who he was talking about it. Same question, different day. "They're fine. Healthy."

And the same motherfucking answer.

Not that Cerviel expected anything different. No doubt his parents were relieved they never had to lay eyes on him again. Ghosts were easier to forgive.

"The chopper will return to the same spot as soon as you give the signal you have the target," Raphael continued. "Or if other…measures were taken."

"Did you call in the rest of the team? More locations in that message."

"They're all in research mode."

"What about Elyon?"

The male arched a brow. "What about her?"

"The last I heard from her, she was infiltrating the Chinese Triad."

"She's fine. Focus on your own work." The leader of the Suits reached out to lay a hand on Cerviel's shoulder. "Good luck."

Cerviel met the male's steady gaze. "I have skills and a bad attitude. I don't need luck."

CHAPTER 2

The puma was glorious. Red and gold under the burnt light of the setting sun. And as it walked down the path, near the water's edge, it sniffed at exotic plants and tall, thick trees. Granted, they weren't exotic to some, but to the puma—to her—life in such a wondrous wild land was as foreign and mysterious as it came.

A soft, summer breeze rushed over her fur. *This is where I belong. This is my home.*

Near the slow-moving water, three cats played on the mossy ground. They turned to look at her, and one, black with green eyes, called to her with a comical, engaging growl. *Play with us. Fight with us.*

She, the red puma, didn't move. She wanted to. Oh, how she wanted to. But something was holding her back. Like a leash on a dog. Though she felt nothing.

We'll protect you, promised the black cat, its emerald eyes flashing with truth and passion. *Find your way here...and we'll protect you.*

Overcome with the desire to join them, she sprang forward, feeling the warm breeze on her puma's face as she took flight. But when she glanced down, around herself, she hadn't gone anywhere. There was only concrete and steel.

She was caught, like a mouse in a trap. Like a prisoner.

Caged.

Caged!

Hallie wrenched her eyes open as an excruciating pain seared the skin of her neck. Instinctively her hand lifted to touch the collar at her throat, only to jerk away before she made contact with the strange metal. She didn't know what the collar was made of, but it was a constant irritant even without the jolt of electricity that was currently running through it.

"Wake up, bitch," a mocking voice called out.

Nostrils flared, Hallie turned her head, her stomach clenching with pure hatred as she caught sight of the man she wished dead every time he descended the narrow flight of stairs into the basement.

He was short and broad with a head that looked too big for his body. There was a small fringe of hair that grimly clung to his bald scalp, and he was wearing a blue suit that had once been perfectly tailored to him, but now strained at the seams. The asshole clearly refused to acknowledge he needed a larger size.

Rick "the Dick" Donaldson.

Meeting his icy blue gaze, Hallie released a low growl deep in her throat. It had taken a few years, but no longer was she afraid of him—no matter what he forced on her, in her. No matter that he kept her naked and seemingly vulnerable. Her hatred fueled her now; every breath, every thought, every plan she concocted late into the night to slice his throat and get the hell out of his cage of misery.

And she would.

Someday, she would.

The man lifted his hand then and Hallie braced herself as he pressed the small device that sent another shock of pain through her body. He laughed his pig squeal laugh as she shuddered. Her hands formed fists and she gritted her teeth against the intensity. He'd get no scream from her.

Fuck him.

Strolling across the cement floor, the arrogant asshole glanced toward the uniformed guard who had risen from his desk in a shadowed corner to stand at attention.

"I have company coming for dinner tonight, Carl. They'll expect to be entertained," he said, waving a hand toward the cage.

"She needs a bath. Every nook and cranny, if you get my meaning. And put her in the harem clothes. Have you fed her?"

Blinking through the unending waves of pain vibrating through her body, Hallie swallowed her fear. She could handle the guard and the *bath* and the goddamn nooks and crannies, but she knew what 'entertaining' Donaldson's guests meant. And she knew if she fought back, bit, punched, spit, as she had in the beginning, he would kill her. Because he almost had. And she wasn't going out like that.

The guard moved forward with a shrug. "She hasn't eaten today."

A snakelike smile curved Donaldson's lips. "Good. I want her hungry. So hungry she'll swallow just about anything." He pressed his face between the bars of the cage. "Do you hear me, animal?" he taunted.

Fury and disgust thundered through her. His neck was so close. Her fingers twitched with need. She had the strength to do it. Easily, in fact, if the collar she wore didn't switch on with any presumed threat and squeeze the life right out of her. She'd tested it twice. So she knew.

His eyes moved down her body, settling on her sex. "You'll be a good girl and open wide. Let Carl get you nice and clean."

Her lip curled. She could practically taste his blood on her tongue. "Fuck. You."

Instead of being angered by her words, he was…excited by them, his watery eyes flickering with heat. "Oh, you will. But not until my guests have been satisfied," he said, blowing her a kiss. "Save your strength, bitch. You're going to need it."

Donaldson glanced toward the guard. "Since this is our last night, I intend to make it one to remember for my guests, but once she's been brought up I want you to start getting things cleaned down here. I was warned there couldn't be anything left that might give our enemies a clue to what makes our…guest so special."

The guard shrugged. "Once it's been disposed of I can start

scrubbing the place. No one will find a damned thing when I'm done."

Hallie frowned. What the hell were they talking about? Last night? Disposed of?

Fear gripped her once again.

An unending nightmare.

Clearly satisfied with the guard's assurances, Donaldson turned to walk away, a bounce in his step. The man who'd abducted her, hurt her, used and abused her with such deep pleasure was the sort of petty, small-dicked, insecure piece of shit who thrived on the misery of others. And the guard, Carl, who was studying her with a disgusted expression, wasn't much better. She didn't know what the man had done in his life to be condemned to spending his days and nights in the basement, but it must have been bad. Or who knew, maybe he got off on it.

Either way, he had very little bite in his bark, and she relished their battles.

Planting his meaty hands on his meatier waist, Carl gave her a look that was supposed to intimidate. "Are you going to behave yourself so I can get you in the shower, or do I need to get the hose?" he demanded.

Hallie bared her teeth. The last time the idiot had come into the cage, she'd taken a small chunk out of his neck. The blood had tasted good, but in retaliation she'd been tied down and beaten black and blue.

Still so worth it.

"Fine." With an impotent glare, he grabbed the nearby hose and turned it on full blast. He aimed the frigid water at Hallie, laughing as she tried to curl away from the ruthless spray. "You like that, bitch? Won't stop until you open up. Get to all those nooks and crannies like the boss says." He moved in closer. "Stupid animal. I could've treated you nice in the shower, but you're the one who wanted to do it the hard way."

"I like the hard way." A male voice echoed through the

basement. "In fact, I prefer it."

The hose was abruptly shut off, allowing Hallie to blink away the water so she could catch sight of the stranger who was calmly walking down the stairs. Breath held and her gut clenched, she readied herself for whatever was coming. Who was he? This stranger with the long, silky black hair and eyes that seemed to glow in the shadows. He was tall and lean, and dressed in jeans and a long, leather duster that made him look like an outlaw. Or a pirate. Her skin hummed with cold, but she forced herself to think, assess. He was good-looking. Too good-looking, with a lean, bronzed face and sculpted features emphasized by a trimmed goatee.

Unfazed by her wet, nude form, she crouched, eyes narrowed, ready for a fight. Was he one of Donaldson's "guests"? Or maybe a new guard? Whoever he was, he'd get nothing from her—not if she was conscious and could use her teeth.

All thoughts took a sharp left as her nostrils flared, and she caught the scent of something she'd never breathed into her lungs before now, but that her body instantly understood and welcomed.

Musk. Raw. Male.

Animal.

It flooded her. Inside and out, and she straightened and then stepped back a foot. As she stared at him, an electric tingle of awareness crawled over her skin, shocking her with its intensity. She didn't know how it was possible, but whatever he was, she was too.

The cat. The puma.

A hum of beautiful unease went through her. Her dreams, the ones she'd had every night for years, weren't just a fantasy. Tears pricked her eyes and she rushed to the bars of the cage, wrapped her fingers around the steel.

Seemingly unaware that he was facing the sort of carnivore that humans should flee from or risk being eaten, Carl tried to pretend he was some kind of dungeon badass. He dropped the hose and placed his hand on the gun holstered at his side.

"Guests aren't allowed down here."

The intruder reached the bottom of the stairs and strolled toward the guard, his movements liquid smooth. "Then it's a good thing I'm not a guest."

The guard scowled, pulling his gun. "Who the hell are you?"

The man's steps never faltered, his smile taunting. "Hmm. Should I say 'your worst nightmare'? It's so clichéd."

Carl nervously swayed from side to side, belatedly feeling the danger that crackled in the air. "Stay back or I'll shoot," he threatened.

"Ah." The stranger lifted his hand to smother a fake yawn. "So we've decided to go with the whole cliché thing."

The guard's pudgy face flushed with fury. "I swear. I'll—"

The words were cut off as the intruder moved with blinding speed. One minute he was standing in front of the guard, and the next he was behind him, his hand knocking away the weapon even as he wrapped his arm around the man's beefy neck. Then he squeezed. Hard.

"Not so brave without the gun in your hand, are you?" he asked.

Carl made a weird, whimpering sound. Like the air being let out of an overinflated balloon.

Hallie didn't know if it was from the lack of oxygen, or pure fear, but she relished it. How many times had he made her feel just as he was feeling now?

"Please," the guard at last managed to rasp. "Tell me what you want."

The stranger's glowing gaze moved toward Hallie. It seemed to take in everything at once. Her long, bedraggled hair. Her exhaustion, her naked body. The bruises. The fierce refusal to show the gnawing terror that was her constant companion.

"I want you to die," the man said, his eyes still pinned to Hallie as he gave a sharp jerk of his arm. There was a loud snap, and just like that the guard's neck was broken. Simple. Efficient. Bye-bye Carl. Then releasing his hold, the stranger allowed the limp body to tumble to the cement floor. "Good boy," he murmured.

Hallie's eyes widened as the man calmly stepped over the dead guard and moved to stand at the door of the cage.

"You're the only prisoner here, correct?"

A toxic combination of fear and a strange, sensual fascination thundered through Hallie. She made a feral noise in her throat, scrambling backward to fold herself in a tight ball. Yes, she felt as if she knew this man. No—her body, her insides, her nose sensed him, understood him. But as he came close, her mind still screamed, warned. Men and pain were too often combined in her world for her not to prepare herself for some new torture.

A dark emotion flared through his eyes as he held up his hands in a gesture of peace.

"Do you speak English?" He waited for her hesitant nod. "Good," he murmured in soothing tones. "Can you walk?"

"Yes," she managed to croak, her eyes widening as he gave a sharp yank on the door of the cage, easily busting the metal lock. He moved forward, the soft leather of his duster rippling around his long legs. "No." She bared her teeth in warning. "Don't come in here."

"It's all right." He halted next to her, crouching down so they were eye to eye. "Easy, kitten. I would die before I harmed you."

Kitten, and the words, and the promise that followed, curled around her like a soft blanket. She didn't know him, but the thing inside her, the cat from her dreams—if it truly existed—did.

"Who are you?" she asked, her legs and hands starting to tremble. With fear? Hunger? She wasn't sure. Maybe both.

"Cerviel," he said.

"Cerviel?" Her brows drew together. She couldn't remember ever hearing a name like that, but it suited him.

"I'm going to get you out of here."

She sucked in a deep breath. Instantly her senses were overwhelmed with his warm male musk, which seemed to utterly permeate the air. Even with the panic thundering through her, she could detect that there was something deeply familiar about this stranger. That the creature inside him was speaking directly to what was inside her. As if it was trying to touch the most primitive part of her.

"There's something different about you," she said. "Familiar. I don't understand it."

"I'm a Pantera," he told her, his nose flaring as he drew in a deep breath. "And I suspect you are as well. Or at least, you have our blood."

Pantera? She'd heard Donaldson and his guests discussing them—puma shifters, he'd said. She'd thought they were insane, but then the dreams had started. Over the years, they'd tried to sound mocking when they spoke of the Pantera, dismissing them as animals, but she hadn't missed the underlying fear in their voices.

She glanced at Carl's lifeless body.

Now she understood why.

"I don't know what I am," she breathed, hissing as he reached out, clearly intending to touch her. "Stop," she growled.

"I need to get that collar off," he said, holding her wary gaze.

Her heart lurched. "You can do that?"

He nodded. "If you'll let me."

Trust had been an elusive bastard in the past five years. But this man was different. Whatever they shared made her defensive instincts ease slightly. She braced herself for his touch. The cringing pain her skin would feel. But as he held the collar in his hands and worked the bolts and locks with a tool he carried, he was shockingly gentle. It was strange, and made her chest tighten, made her eyes fill with tears, but when his fingers brushed her neck as he worked, she didn't want to jerk away. Instead, she wanted to lean into him. Closer. Absorb his warmth, his protection.

She wanted to…

Purr.

Not in a sexual way. No. This wave of feeling, of intimacy, was on a deeper, almost cellular level. Like ocean wave meeting warm sand. Meant to connect.

A groan escaped her lips as the heavy, oppressive collar was lifted from her neck and tossed away.

"We'd better go," he said, moving back, crawling out of the cage.

Hallie rubbed her throat, raw from being imprisoned for so long. "I need a sheet or a towel. I can't go out like this. Anything will do."

"How's this?" He grabbed a bag from the bottom of the stairs. She hadn't seen him carrying it. Inside was a pair of sweats, a hoodie and wool-lined boots. "Might be a little big. Didn't know your size."

"It's perfect. Thank you." She dressed quickly, then crawled out of the cage.

On her own.

For the first time in five years.

CHAPTER 3

Cradling the exhausted and far too thin female in his arms, Cerviel's gaze swept the basement, assessing.

"Hold tight, kitten, I'm going to get you out of here," he said, eyeing the stairs.

He wasn't sure how long he'd been there. Longer than he'd intended, that was for sure. Not like him. Not like him at all.

As if to prove the point he heard the sounds of muffled voices and doors opening and closing upstairs. No doubt Donaldson's guests were arriving. Which meant the sooner he could get them out of there, the better.

Crossing the cement floor, he was brought to a halt when Hallie stiffened in his arms.

"Wait," she whispered.

He frowned down at her. "What?"

She pointed toward a narrow door that he'd assumed was a storage closet.

"Go out the service door," she said. "No one ever uses it."

Flashing her a grateful smile, Cerviel spun on his heel and headed straight for the opposite end of the basement. The female was as resourceful as she was courageous.

And beautiful.

Exquisitely beautiful.

Not that he should even be looking. She was an asset, nothing more. Not to mention she'd been through hell on earth, and what she required now was peace and protection.

Moving with a silence no human could match, he reached the door and gave it a sharp yank. It swung open, revealing a narrow pathway that led toward a side road.

Outside, night had descended, but the monstrous ranch house that was constructed almost entirely of glass allowed light to spill out in a circle that encompassed the entire yard. Not good. That meant they were going to be exposed for at least a hundred feet.

Tucking Hallie even closer to his body, he focused his gaze on the long, wooden stables. If he could get to the outbuilding without being spotted, they might have a chance of escaping unnoticed.

Again he heard voices, footfall. Darting forward, he took off, using the most direct route to the stables.

Unfortunately, one of the numerous guards patrolling the grounds rounded the corner of the house just as he stepped into a pool of light. There was a shout of warning, then the loud crack of a rifle being fired.

Cerviel hunched his shoulders, using his body to protect the female tucked against his chest. He thought he heard her mumble something about leaving her behind so he could escape. But he ignored it. He recalled Raphael's orders about lighting the place up if he couldn't get to her, or something went down. Hours ago, he'd thought nothing of it. Would've followed through in a heartbeat— or the quick strike of a match. But now…this female… She'd changed things. In him, and in this situation. No matter what his direct orders had been, he was pretty motherfucking sure he couldn't have possibly let her die with Donaldson.

Not good.

Ghosts weren't supposed feel.

Neither empathy, nor rage.

Both of which he'd felt as he'd stood in the shadows at the top of the stairs, listening the onetime congressman talk about passing Hallie around to his guests like a party favor. It took everything he'd had to not rip the male apart right then. But Hallie was the mission, the priority.

The next time Cerviel crossed paths with the human, however—he intended to gut him. A fact he wouldn't be sharing with Raphael. Too bad he had no access to his puma outside the Wildlands. His cat would enjoy a good hunt to kill. He could feel the beast's hunger vibrating beneath his skin even now.

"Watch out," the female called as a smattering of gunfire erupted around them.

Running in a zigzag pattern, Cerviel hissed as one of the bullets sliced through the flesh of his upper arm. It wasn't a serious injury, but it hurt like a bitch. And worse, the drops of blood that hit the dry, barren ground would allow the guards to follow their trail.

At least they wouldn't be able to scent him.

Picking up speed, he hauled ass to the stables. Finally reaching them, he darted around the edge of the wooden structure and carefully lowered Hallie to the ground. She was exhausted, shivering, her hair still wet. Goddess knew how long it had been since she'd eaten anything. Any hope of a stealthy getaway was well and truly over. Now he needed a distraction so he wouldn't have to deal with Donaldson's considerable security staff.

"Stay here," he commanded, reaching into the pocket of his coat to pull out a small handgun. "Shoot anyone who isn't me."

She bit her lower lip, her gaze moving to the tear in his leather duster. "You're injured."

"Nothing that won't heal." He glared at his arm. "But the asshole who shot me is going to pay. This is my favorite coat."

She gave a choked laugh, a completely strange sound in the moment they found themselves in. "You killed a guard, saw me wet and naked and abused, and were shot. Doesn't anything ever bother you?"

A rueful smile touched his lips and his eyes connected with hers. "Seeing you caged and collared like an animal. That bothered the fuck out of me."

"Well, aren't I?" she returned without heat, then raised an eyebrow at him. "An animal?"

His jaw tightened and though his voice remained barely above a whisper, it was fierce. "You are Pantera, female. You're never ever going to be caged or collared again. Only to be respected and…"

"And what?"

He pointed a warning finger at her. "Stay here and don't make a sound," he commanded.

"Where are you going?" she whispered, clutching the gun in her right hand.

His brows lifted and his mouth quirked with a wicked grin. "To play the Pied Piper."

Without giving her time to argue, Cerviel turned and headed back into the spray of bullets. A landscape he was totally at ease within—mild to moderate chaos. Two guards were running toward the stables, one of them shooting and the other screaming into a walkie-talkie.

As he'd hoped, they instantly charged after him, calling out all sorts of vile shit and shooting wildly. Without having to worry about Hallie, Cerviel easily avoided being hit, his speed putting distance between him and his pursuers.

He was across the circular driveway when there was a shout from the main house and Donaldson abruptly appeared on the wide terrace with several men dressed in expensive suits. The cat inside him scratching to be released, Cerviel battled the instinct to turn back and have a painful, deliciously lethal chat with the congressman and his friends.

Later, he promised the puma through gritted, ready teeth.

For now, he had to get Hallie to safety, then to Raphael.

Careful not to lose the growing crowd of guards, he angled though the small rose garden and down the sloping trail that would eventually lead to the Salt River that flowed through the barren landscape.

It would be the logical way to flee from the ranch.

Less than ten minutes later he could hear the muffled grunts and groans from the guards as they wearily climbed over the slick rocks and splashed through the small eddies of freezing cold water.

He glanced back, judging that he was far enough away to double back.

Crouching low to the ground, he headed straight up the steep bank. He leaped from boulder to boulder, his catlike quickness allowing him to disappear without making a sound. Then, following the line of the barbed-wire fence, he cautiously made his way back to Hallie.

* * *

Hallie forced herself to stay hidden behind the stables.

In her mind, she wanted to be Xena, Warrior Princess, a show she'd seen Carl watching from time to time on the small TV hung in the corner of the basement. She hated this. It was embarrassing to cower like a weakling in the darkness while Cerviel risked his life to rescue her. But even as she considered how she could help, a voice in the back of her mind warned that taking such a foolish risk would not only endanger herself, but Cerviel.

She was weak from hunger, and her body hadn't fully recovered from her most recent beating.

Until she could regain her strength, she wasn't going to be able to do anything but stay out of the way.

Clutching the gun in one hand, she made herself take deep, even breaths, concentrating on counting each passing second. It was the only way to leash the nervous energy that squeezed her heart and made her palms sweat. She'd just reached seven hundred and fifty when she caught the scent of warm musk.

"Don't shoot," a low male voice commanded.

Cerviel.

A form appeared in the shadows. Silent. Graceful.

Relief and awareness flooded through her as her strange ability to see in the dark revealed the full impact of his stern features and the lethal glow of power in his eyes.

Her heart missed a beat as he leaned down to scoop her up into his arms. With astonishing ease, he straightened and cradled her gently against his chest as he jogged away from the ranch.

His unnerving strength should have terrified her. She'd been beaten and abused by men who were willing to starve or even drug her, until she couldn't fight to protect herself. But somehow she felt deeply and inexplicably comforted as she snuggled against the broad chest of this man. Or *male*, as she'd heard Donaldson and the others say. It was as if she was going to be protected for the first time in her life.

With a shake of her head, she allowed her tense muscles to relax, and shoved the gun into the front pocket of her hoodie. She wasn't used to weapons. Which meant she was more likely to shoot herself or Cerviel than any enemy. But she was a quick study, and glad to have it. In case.

She wasn't going back to that basement, or that cage.

End. Of. Story.

She circled her arms around his neck as he raced over the hard, dusty ground. She didn't understand why she knew bone-deep that she could trust this male, that he was the complete antithesis of Donaldson. But for now, she was simply going to appreciate being out of the cage and running away from the men who'd made her existence a living hell. Soon enough, she'd have to think about where she would go, live. How she would take care of herself…

Remaining silent as Cerviel vaulted over a wooden gate, she strained for any sounds of pursuit. But she couldn't hear anything over the pounding of her heart. Fear? Wonder? Relief?

Maybe all three.

At last she glanced over his broad shoulder, ensuring that none of Donaldson's guards were in pursuit. She didn't see anyone. Still, she forced herself to wait until they at last reached the foothills before she asked the question that was burning on the tip of her tongue.

"Where are we going?"

He smoothly moved up the steep incline, leaping over boulders without breaking a sweat.

"We need a place to lie low until I can contact my people and arrange a transport out of here," he told her.

"Your people?" Her heart leapt into her throat. What was she going to be forced to do next? Could they be trusted? And if so, would she be able to remain with them for a short time to figure out what she was going to do next?

"The Pantera," he said as he slowed his ruthless pace as they reached the line of pine trees.

A strange sensation tingled deep inside her. Again. So similar to the one she had in her dreams. And when this male had moved down the stairs back at the ranch, and stalked toward her cage. She glanced up and studied his lean, beautiful, fierce face, wishing she had the nerve to reach up and trace the elegant lines of his features.

"You can change into a cat?" she asked him.

"A puma," he corrected. "And only in the Wildlands."

She'd heard of that place. Donaldson had mentioned it, but without details. "Where is it? The Wildlands?"

"Deep in the bayous of Louisiana. It's beautiful." His mouth curved into an easy smile. "You'll love it. So green and lush, the slow-moving water setting the pace. You'll find that our people have generous hearts and are always ready and willing to give you and your puma the friendship and support that has been clearly lacking in your life."

With her trust issues, his words should've troubled her. Or at the very least, made her suspicious. But they didn't. Just the opposite, in fact. She was fascinated by the world he spoke of— and strangely comforted by the idea of others like her offering support and kindness. Even if it was for a short time.

"But I'm not Pantera," she said. "I'm human. Same with my parents."

"Perhaps you were born a human."

Prickles of heat moved over her skin. She swallowed tightly.

"Something changed," he continued. "Your blood—"

"You suspect I have Pantera blood?"

"Yes." His glowing gaze lowered, studying her face with a fierce intensity. "I can smell it."

She arched a brow at him. "Are you saying I smell?"

His nose flared and he inhaled, the heat of his body wrapping around her like a caress. "Oh yeah, you smell, kitten. And it's glorious."

She shuddered at his words, at the way he'd spoken them, while new, terrifying sensations swirled through her. She had Pantera blood inside her? How? How was that even possible?

She forced her mind back, but it only fell into darkness.

She growled to herself, and abruptly turned away from his burning gaze. She couldn't process her strange reaction to this male or what he'd said. Not after what she'd been through. It wasn't true. Couldn't be, and yet...

"I've always known there was something different about me," she said almost to herself. "Why else would I have been taken, locked up..."

"Not different," Cerviel said. "Superior."

She smiled at his words, a moment of lightness, pressing her head tight against his chest as he pushed his way through a wall of pine branches illuminated by the half-moon's light. The landscape was becoming increasingly remote and untamed. The sort of place humans rarely visited. The sort of place where an animal might be very comfortable.

"You don't lack in confidence," she pointed out.

He laughed softly. "No. I'm sure many would call me an arrogant bastard."

She glanced up at him.

"In fact, my Pantera brothers have called me much worse." He gave her a wink.

The action went straight through her and penetrated her heart.

The one that had broken, then had ceased to beat during her time in the cage. He was something. Dangerous and sexy, yet held so much warmth and kindness within him. Her eyes searched his, so dark and liquid. He was one of the good guys. She was certain of it. Just as she was suddenly certain she would do anything to get him to smile at her again.

She swallowed thickly, feeling oddly vulnerable. "Do you have a big family?"

As a quick breeze picked up around them, he ducked beneath a low overhang and followed a narrow path that led along a deepening ravine.

"Hundreds."

She blinked. Had she heard him right? "Hundreds?"

He slowed as the path narrowed. On one side was a wall of rock, on the other a sheer drop-off. She gripped him a little tighter.

"My pack is my family," he told her, though his voice held a thread of sadness as he said it.

"That must be nice." Envy speared her heart. She couldn't imagine being surrounded by a large, loving pack. She'd been alone for so, so long.

He glanced down at her, his brows pulled together. "Have you always been at the ranch?"

"I…" Her words trailed away as she gave a helpless shake of her head. "I don't know."

His frown deepened. "What do you mean?"

She hated having to tell him this. It made her feel so damn weak. "I think something was done to me," she admitted, her gut clenching with both pain and sickness as she tried to push back in time. "I can't remember anything before waking up in that cage five years ago."

He looked stunned. "Nothing?"

She shook her head. "It's blank. It's as if my mind was erased." She regarded him with somber, pensive eyes. "It's as if I never   existed."

CHAPTER 4

It was a nearly impossible task, but Cerviel bit back his urge to press Hallie for more details on her loss of memory. There was only one reason to clear someone's mind. And that was because they had information that would be dangerous.

But right now he needed to concentrate on finding a place to keep her safe from Donaldson. At least until he could make sure it was safe to signal for the chopper and they could get the hell out of Wyoming.

Following the curve of the narrow pathway, he discovered a wide opening that led into a cave. It was shallow, with a low ceiling and a smooth rock floor, but it was well away from the human pathways, and best of all, no one could approach from behind or below. He could easily defend the location.

"I think we should be safe here," he murmured, ducking inside and crouching down to settle Hallie near the back of the space.

He was about to straighten when she reached out to grab his arm.

"Are you leaving?"

The slight panic in her voice made his gut clench. "I want to do a sweep and make sure there's no one who might stumble across this cave. Also want to make sure our tracks are covered." He eyed her seriously. "You still have the gun?"

"Yes." She reached into the front pocket of her hoodie to pull out the Taurus PT111.

He grimaced. She held the weapon like it was a snake about to bite her.

"Shoot first and ask questions later," he commanded in stern tones. "Got it?"

Perhaps sensing his lack of confidence, Hallie squared her shoulders and gripped the gun with far more determination.

"Got it."

Cerviel hesitated. He hated to leave her alone. She was clearly feeling vulnerable and exposed. No big surprise for a female who'd been locked in a cage for years.

But he had to make sure they weren't being followed.

Dipping his head, he brushed a reassuring kiss over her furrowed brow. Then, with a sharp movement, he was on his feet and heading out of the cave.

He didn't use the pathway, however. Instead he scrambled up the vertical rocky slope and circled around the peak of the ridge. Once near the top, he pulled out his cellphone that had been boosted by Xavier just in case there was no signal and hit Raphael's number.

"I've got the asset," he said as soon as he heard the older male's voice.

"Alive?" Raphael demanded.

"Yeah, but she's been—" Cerviel bit off his words. He couldn't think about what'd been done Hallie. Not unless he wanted to risk everything by returning to the ranch and slicing Rick Donaldson into bloody strips. "Have you figured out why it was so important that you sent me to retrieve her?"

"Not yet. Why?"

"Are you still willing to let her die if you decide she's a threat to a Pantera?"

"Sacrifices are always demanded. You know that better than anyone, Cerviel."

"Maybe you won't get her back, then," he said impulsively.

There was a low snarl over the line, then, "Cerviel—"

"She's been tortured, for fuck's sake. She has no idea where she came from or why. I won't have her hurt again."

The leader of the Pantera exhaled heavily, didn't say anything for a few seconds. When he finally did, his tone was calm and controlled. "Do you trust my word?"

Cerviel didn't hesitate. "Yes."

"You get her back to us and I swear to you she won't be harmed in any way. But you get that you sound more like her mate than a member of the PSL, right?"

Cerviel refused to answer. In fact, he refused to even think on the male's ridiculous observation. All he wanted was to keep an innocent female safe. "I'll bring her in."

"Is that the only reason you're calling? Or are you ready for the evac?" Raphael asked.

Cerviel considered. He glanced around the thick layers of trees and rugged terrain. He was fairly certain he'd managed to shake off his pursuers. But if the guards were still searching for them, the approaching lights and sound of a chopper would most certainly pinpoint their location.

Especially if he had to travel with Hallie to a spot where the chopper could easily land.

"No. Call it off for tonight. I don't want to alert the guards where we are," he told Raphael. "We'll meet at the same coordinates where I was dropped off, at dawn."

"I'll let the pilot know," Raph promised. "But remember, he'll be on the ground for ten minutes. Not a second longer. You need to be there."

"Got it."

Ending the connection, Cerviel slid the phone into his pocket and set off at a rapid pace. He did a careful sweep to make sure there were no stray campers in the area before returning to the pathway to make certain there were no footprints that might reveal the direction they'd taken.

Once confident he'd left nothing behind that could lead the guards to the cave, he headed toward a hunting lodge he'd seen when the chopper had dropped him off three hours ago. The four human men who were staying at the large, log structure were still awake, but not one of them noticed the silent shadow that slid through the back door. They were on the porch, busy swapping bullshit about the 'one that got away' and drinking heavily from a bottle of scotch.

Collecting what he wanted, Cerviel left as silently as he'd arrived, melting into the shadows with the ease of a predator.

A quarter of an hour later, he was back at the cave.

"It's me," he called out before stepping into the opening.

The last thing he wanted was to startle Hallie. She might not know much about guns, but she could squeeze a trigger and put a bullet through his heart.

"I promise not to shoot," she called out.

An odd sensation twisted his heart. The light, almost teasing words couldn't disguise the aching relief he could hear in her voice.

Entering the cave, he moved to settle next to her shivering body, setting up a small battery-powered lantern before placing a canvas bag between them on the floor.

"I come bearing gifts."

With a lift of her brows, Hallie watched in silence as he pulled out the loaf of bread, a large container of roast beef and a bag of chips. Hardly gourmet fare, but he'd overheard the guard telling Donaldson that he hadn't fed Hallie. Right now any food would no doubt taste like ambrosia to her.

"Where did you get this?" she demanded in appreciative surprise.

"I borrowed it from a hunting lodge a few miles away."

She glanced up to study his overly-innocent smile. "You borrowed it, huh?"

He shrugged. "Something like that."

"Did you poach it?"

"Does it matter?"

"Hell no," she admitted on a laugh. "I'm starving."

He laughed with her as she reached to take the bread. She

quickly assembled two sandwiches, piling them high with roast beef. Not that he was going to complain. He was a carnivore. The more meat the better.

Taking the sandwich that she offered him, Cerviel absently consumed it in four large bites. Then, leaning against the wall of the cave, he studied his companion in the warm, soft light of the lantern with unconcealed fascination.

She was so exquisite. From her wide, hazel eyes to the long, thick red hair that bracketed her lovely face with such smooth skin and pure lines. But it wasn't her physical beauty that attracted his attention, and made him—in Raphael's words—act like a mate where she was concerned. It was the unbroken strength he could see in her eyes, and the courageous spirit visible in the aura that flickered around her.

She was a warrior.

She was a survivor.

Fuck… He scrubbed a hand over his face. He could only hope that the Pantera's need to know the truth didn't do irreparable harm to his tenuous yet ever-growing bond with her.

Polishing off the last of her sandwich with more restraint than he'd displayed, Hallie glanced up to discover his unwavering gaze.

"What?" She put her fingers to her mouth, then her nose. "Do I have something on my face?"

Unable to resist temptation, Cerviel reached out to lightly stroke a finger over her cheek. *Damn.* Her skin was as silky smooth as it looked. And now that she had some food in her belly, a hint of color was replacing her unnatural pallor.

Her hand dropped from her face, and her lips parted in an unconscious invitation, but with a heroic effort, he managed to resist temptation.

"Your face is perfect," he assured her, pulling his fingers from her cheek. *She doesn't belong to you, Cerviel. No female ever can. She is yours to protect.*

For now.

For tonight.

She continued to study him. "What's wrong? Is your arm still hurting you?"

He didn't know if it was a good or bad thing that she seemed to be able to read his moods. Usually it took people years to see beneath his glib façade. If at all.

"My arm's already healed," he told her with a slight, and possibly cocky, grin. "The beauty of Pantera blood."

She arched a brow. "So what is it?"

"If you're willing, I'd like to see if I can retrieve your earlier memories," he said.

She stiffened, her eyes widening with alarm. "Why?" she breathed.

Cerviel grimaced. He hated to press her when it was obvious she was unnerved by the thought of resurrecting her old memories. Unfortunately, he knew if he didn't convince her to let him coax her past the block in her mind, Raphael might just insist that one of the Healers be given the opportunity to try when they returned to the Wildlands.

And the thought of anyone else being so intimately connected to her…

His inner puma snarled with a savage protest.

Nope. That wasn't going to happen. Unleashing Raphael's feral temper sounded pretty shitty, but Cerviel would share whatever information—strike that, whatever *pertinent* information —he gleaned from the extraction.

He cleared the growl from his voice. His mind—no, his cat was starting to take over his reason. Dangerous for a member of The Six. They survived on rules, following orders, never going rogue no matter how desperately they wished to. He needed to get his act together and face reality. This female didn't belong to him. He was there to find and retrieve only. Then he walked the hell away.

Back into the shadows where all ghosts live.

But, memory extraction… It could help. Not only her, but the mission.

He glanced up at her. "I think your past, and what happened in it, what brought you to this point, might be important," he said in cautious tones.

Her exquisite face clouded with uneasiness, and maybe even a touch of distrust. "Is that why you came for me?" she demanded. "Because of something in my past?"

Cerviel hesitated. His first instinct was to comfort her with a lie. Only the knowledge she would be far more pissed at learning he hadn't been honest with her forced the truth past his lips.

"We didn't know you existed until we intercepted a message from our enemies that listed the name of this ranch."

She stared at him warily. "Still, you believe I have information you need?"

He couldn't help himself. Desperate to comfort her, desperate to quell any sign that she didn't believe his heart was pure where her safety and security was concerned, he reached for her again, this time cupping her cheek with his palm. "It's possible. But trust me, Hallie, it wouldn't have mattered if you had information or not." His eyes never left hers for a moment. "Nothing could've stopped me from rescuing you."

Or protecting you…

Caring for you.

Wanting you.

Not even a direct order from my leader.

CHAPTER 5

Hallie had never been this physically close to a male before and not felt fear, hatred and a desperate need to kill.

But Cerviel wasn't just any male.

The dark-eyed, dark-haired puma shifter made her feel something else altogether. Something she hadn't felt in...forever, it seemed. A new and amazing sensation.

Safety.

And when he spoke about her past, her memories...she believed he was speaking the truth. Her shoulders fell as she gazed at him. That wasn't just wishful thinking, was it? Or a reaction to being rescued? She truly wanted to believe that there were people out there who cared if she was alive or dead. More than cared. Even if they were complete strangers.

But that didn't make it any less unnerving to think about having her memories forced back to the surface.

After all, she had to be repressing them for a reason. Her gut tightened painfully. What if they were too traumatic for her to deal with? What if she lost it in front of him? Broke down in tears that never ceased?

"I don't know about this," she whispered, her tone husky.

They were so close, maybe five or six inches apart as they gazed into each other's eyes. Cerviel slipped a finger beneath her chin and tilted her face up so he could study her wary expression.

"Tell me what's bothering you, kitten," he urged.

Warmth spread through her at the word, the...endearment, and all her fears and self-doubt eased. "I'm afraid."

"Of me?" Something that might have been disappointment

flared through his eyes. "I swear on my life I won't harm you."

"Oh no." She gave a sharp shake of her head. "I'm not afraid of you."

The tension lifted from his beautiful face. "Then what?"

She bit her bottom lip, wishing for one brief second that it was his teeth there, not her own. "I'm just worried… What if…"

He allowed his thumb to brush the line of her jaw as her words trailed away.

"What if?" he prompted softly.

"What if there's something terrible in my past?"

She watched as Cerviel's brows furrowed, his thumb continuing to stroke a tender caress up and down her jaw.

"*Ma chère*, you've already endured terrible. You've been through hell and it's only made you stronger," he said, his eyes so intense on her own, she had to remind herself to breathe. "Like finely tempered steel."

She laughed softly. Right now she didn't feel like finely tempered anything. She felt raw and fragile. As if she might shatter into a million pieces, never to recover. She felt like she never wanted him more than three feet away from her at any given time.

"I don't mean something that was done to me." She struggled to explain her reluctance. "Like you said, I've been through hell. But I can deal with that. I've made my peace with that." She felt her eyes prick with tears, and hated herself for them. For the weakness that five years in captivity inflicted on a person.

Or to a Pantera?

"Hallie…" he began with gentleness.

She shook her head. "What if I've done something to someone else? Something unforgivable."

He stilled, perhaps sensing there was more to her words than some vague, unexplainable fear. "Why would you think that?"

She licked her dry lips, glancing toward the opening of the cave. Logically she knew there wasn't a guard hovering just out of sight, but the awareness of being constantly watched was too ingrained to be easily dismissed.

At last satisfied that they were alone, she returned her attention to the man seated next to her on the hard ground.

"I overheard Donaldson talking to his boss on the phone," she said.

It was as if a switch had been flipped, and Cerviel turned from tender beast to a fierce male on the edge. "What was his boss's name?"

She paused, allowing the conversation to rewind in her head. It'd occurred shortly after she'd awakened at the ranch. "I think it was Benton," she said, only to wrinkle her nose. "Or maybe Benson. Something like that."

Cerviel's breath hissed through his teeth, as if he recognized the name. "Can you tell me what Donaldson said?"

"Does this Benson person have to do with why you came to get me?"

"Please, Hallie."

The almost desperate tone in his voice had her pressing on. Granted, she wasn't abandoning her query, just backing off it for a moment. "He said that he was keeping me safe, and promised that nothing bad would ever happen to me." Her lip curled with utter disgust. *Safe. Yeah, right.* One day she was going to return to the ranch, and keep Donaldson 'safe.' "That piece of shit liar."

"Agreed." Fire crackled in Cerviel's eyes and he looked murderous. "Anything else?"

"He said that he understood I was special," she said on a bitter snarl. "And that I was vital to the success of his boss's plans. He assured Benson that he would do whatever necessary to keep me alive."

Cerviel's eyes, dark and foreboding, were pinned to hers as his fingers were softly caressing her jaw, making her breathing uneven. He was clearly absorbing her words, silently running them through his clever mind. Hallie was beginning to realize that this man was the sort who didn't impulsively leap to conclusions, or rashly strike out. Even with a beast inside him, he was a thinker. He was a man who considered a problem, or enemy, very carefully, and then chose the most effective means of destruction.

Not that she didn't assume he couldn't be provoked into savage violence. A puma dwelled inside him, after all.

But she knew his cold logic was far more dangerous than fangs and claws.

"Answer *my* question now," she said, trying to keep herself focused as he touched her.

He paused for only a moment before nodding. "Benson is an enemy of the Pantera. One of our most vicious adversaries." As his fingers traced the pulse at her neck, his gaze roamed over her face, landing gently on her mouth. "We intercepted a message on his private cellphone. It was about you and your location."

"What about it?" she asked, her skin humming with awareness and heat. "To get me? Rescue me?"

He said nothing. And his intense but secret expression warned her she would get no more from him. Not that she would stop trying. She was owed the truth.

"Why does that conversation make you fear your past?" he asked, his eyes finding hers once again. "Between Benson and Donaldson?"

"Because it's obvious that I have some connection to these assholes. I was selected for some particular reason. Maybe it has to do with something I did when I was young." Her stomach rolled, killing the safe, almost sensual feeling she'd been having since they'd shared their stolen meal. "Or something to do with my family. A part of me senses that my life is easier not remembering."

He slowly nodded. "I get that."

She released a shaky sigh. "Yeah, right."

"I'm serious, kitten." He allowed his hand to slide from her throat. Hallie immediately missed the warmth of his touch. Where physical contact had always been a nightmare, something to fear and fight against and recoil from, with Cerviel, it was almost medicinal, helping to ease the anxious ball of dread in the pit of her stomach. While awakening something she no longer thought existed inside her. Attraction.

"I've spent a lot of years wishing that I could erase the memories of my past," he continued thoughtfully.

Her lips parted in surprise. "Why?"

"My sister died."

She sucked in a breath at his blunt confession. "I'm so sorry," she breathed, reaching out for his hand. It was big and warm and strong. Like him. "Was it an accident?"

"No." His eyes grew distant, his features hardening.

With pain? Anger? Guilt? Probably a toxic combination of all three.

"It was close to the time of our festival," he said. "It's always marked by the bloom of the Dyesse lily."

Hallie furrowed her brow. "I've never heard of that flower."

"It grows only in the Wildlands," he said, his voice thick with emotion. "One day I hope you'll see it. My sister wanted me to go with her to try and find the first bloom, but I told her no. I was too busy training with my friends to be bothered with an annoying little sister. I was such an ass."

She squeezed his fingers, feeling his pain, and he squeezed back. "You don't have to say any more, Cerviel."

He slowly shook his head, his unfocused eyes revealing that he was still lost in the past. "I don't mind telling you," he insisted. "It's so much easier trying to keep my memories of her locked away, good and bad, you know? But that's not fair to her. She deserves to be remembered."

Hallie had this intense need to not only comfort him, but to get as close to him as possible. Crawl into his lap and wrap her arms around him and bury her face in his neck. But she didn't dare. Firstly, because she didn't want him to continue to see her as that victim in the cage. She wanted him to see her strong and capable.

And also because maybe...maybe he had someone. Maybe there was a lucky female waiting for him back in the Wildlands, and she had no right...

Just the idea of it made her belly clench painfully. And there was something else too...something that lived beneath her ribs that disliked the notion of Cerviel and another female even more than she did.

Was it possible that she had more than just Pantera blood? Was it possible that a real and true and fierce cat hummed beneath her breasts?

"Talk to me," Hallie said with gentle sincerity. "I'd love to know about her."

He glanced up, his eyes betraying a soul-deep vulnerability. "Yeah?"

She nodded.

He took a moment, as if gathering his thoughts. "Her name was Evie," he started, his expression melting with a fond affection. The sort of affection that Hallie deeply envied. Had anyone ever thought about her with such love? She gave a small shake of her head, forcing herself to concentrate on Cerviel's low words. "She was a pesky, crazy, fun, incredibly charming thing who was always tumbling into trouble." He laughed, but it was a melancholy sound. "There was no dare she wouldn't take, and no lengths she wouldn't go to, to make people smile. She was like a ray of sunshine whenever she appeared."

"She sounds amazing," Hallie breathed.

His eyes connected with hers. "She was."

Long seconds passed. "What happened?" she at last prompted.

"Our homeland is deep in the bayous of Louisiana and heavily protected by magic," he said, his eyes darkening with emotion. "Or at least we all assumed it was protected. What we didn't know at the time was that a jealous goddess had been secretly destroying the layers of protection we'd taken for granted forever." He released a harsh sigh. "Evie was at the edge of the Wildlands when she was shot by poachers. She should have been able to heal, but the bullets tore straight through her heart and she bled to death before I found her."

Horror flooded through Hallie. Not only for the young girl whose life was ended way too early, but for the family left behind to mourn her loss.

She glanced up. Into the face of the male before her. He was all sharp angles, and misery swimming in the dark depths of his eyes. He blamed himself. Still. And she could see that the guilt of failing his sister had clearly shaped his life, defining him in a way he probably didn't even realize.

"Oh, Cerviel." She impulsively leaned forward to place a kiss on the hard line of his jaw. "It wasn't your fault."

When she pulled back, his eyes met hers. "It doesn't matter if it was or wasn't," he said, the threads of sadness in his voice tugging at her heart. "It feels like it's my fault. Every minute of every day."

"I'm sure your parents helped you—"

"They believed it, too."

Shock flew through her. "No…"

"It's all right. It's done. It's why I left, accepted our leader's call and became…this."

"This? What is *this*?"

He shook his head, and she thought she'd lost him. That maybe he was going to shut down, shut off and tell her he couldn't tell her anything. But when he found her gaze again, his eyes betrayed not only a deep pain, but a desperate need to connect. If just for a moment.

"I'm essentially a ghost, Hallie. To everyone, my parents included. I don't exist."

Her brows knit together. "What do you mean?"

"To everyone, except a select few, I'm dead." His jaw hardened. "That's all I can tell you. Frankly, it's more than I should be telling you."

She gaped at him. He wasn't serious. Why would he seek out something like that? A position like that? Even as she thought the question, she knew the answer. His sister was dead. It was only fitting that he was too, in the only way that worked.

Her heart squeezed with pain. It was universal, the language of loss.

"Trust me," he said as the air inside the cave grew suddenly colder. "It's better this way. Better for them."

"You may believe that—"

"I *know* that."

"Stop. Don't say any more." The words came out in a rush, and without thought or good sense, she leaned in and kissed him. One simple, gentle kiss, then another until he was silent, except the catch of his breath.

She had zero experience, just instinct. But she not only had to make him stop talking, she had to prove to him that he was very much alive. And wanted.

"Hallie," he uttered on a low growl against her lips.

Believing that the animal-like sound was a call for more, she smiled and leaned in to kiss him again. But he pulled back and cursed viciously.

Heat surged into Hallie's cheeks. Oh god... She wanted to melt into the floor. Embarrassment and shame spiraled through her and she sat back on her butt and groaned. "I'm so sorry."

"Don't be," he insisted.

She stared at the rock and dirt floor, illuminated by the lantern. She couldn't look at him. "I wasn't thinking—"

"Hallie—"

"If you have a girlfriend, or god, a wife—"

She heard movement, then his hands were on her, warm, heavy palms on either side of her face. "Look at me." His tone forced her chin up and her eyes to meet his. "Listen," he said in a fierce voice. "I belong to no one. I have no mate. Your kiss"—his gaze dropped to her mouth and his nostrils flared—"was my heaven on earth. My mind is gone and my body is pulsing with a need I never even knew existed. But I don't want to… Shit. After what you've been through…you deserve—"

Understanding finally dawned, and she cut him off quickly. "Hey. Wait a second. That's my choice."

He stared at her, wary, hungry.

"I decide what I deserve…*male.*" She punctuated the word. Wanting him to see her certainty, her strength, her resolve.

Dark eyebrows lifted over even darker eyes. "I'm just saying that perhaps you should focus for a moment on the past, knowing the truth and settling it, before you start on…" As he searched for the right words, those eyes flashed with a fire that was barely contained. "The future."

She inhaled sharply as a soft hum vibrated around her heart. *Future.* Was he actually suggesting they might see each other after all of this? Would the ghost actually allow himself to be resurrected for her?

Stop.

"Listen to me, kitten," he continued, staring deeply into her eyes. "The passing years have helped to ease the pain of losing Evie, but it still isn't easy." His gaze searched hers intently. "Just as facing your own past won't be easy. But the truth—"

"Will set me free?" she finished for him, her brow lifting.

He gave her a halfhearted smile. "Something like that."

She drew in a slow, shaky breath. Forget the future, planning for it or praying for it. Maybe he was right. Maybe she needed to know, deal with what had come before so she could see a clear path ahead. A real path. Hell, if Cerviel could endure the gnawing regret and guilt at the death of his sister, she could find the courage to rip aside the barriers and peer at what was behind them.

However disturbing it might turn out to be…

"You know how to do this?" she asked him. "Take me back?"

He nodded. "It's not a perfect science, but I'll do my best."

"And you'll stay with me?" she demanded.

"I'm not going anywhere, kitten," he said, his words sounding like a pledge. Like something that went beyond the moment.

Something that spoke directly to her heart.

With a hiss she released the breath she'd been holding. "Okay. Let's do it."

CHAPTER 6

His training had been lengthy and in-depth. As it should be. To extract truth or memories from the mind was no easy feat. In Cerviel's experience, humans fell under the weight of regression therapy far more easily than Pantera. So he'd wondered how Hallie would respond as he'd guided her through the initial calming meditation. What part of her would take hold as the suggestions were offered—how much puma blood did she have within her?

Under the glow of the small lantern, Cerviel stared down at her, lying on her back on a bed of leaves. Eyes closed, face relaxed, she breathed easily. This beautiful female he'd guided into a deep trance. This female who trusted him. Who'd kissed him... Who had more Pantera within her than he'd guessed. It had taken almost an hour to bring her to the state she was in, and he needed to move quickly.

"With each exhale, Hallie," he said in a slow, soothing voice, "I want you to release all the stress and tension that has built up inside you."

Her lips parted and her inhalations grew deeper, while her exhalations were slow and weighty.

"That's right. Every sound you hear, every breath you take sends you deeper within yourself." He waited for a few seconds, watching her, assessing. "Very good, Hallie. Now, I want you to go back, back...follow the trail through the trees. And as you do, you'll see each year ticking by. Stop when you've reached five." He waited for several seconds, wanting to make sure he saw flickers of movement on her eyelids. "Good. Now, just observe what's around you without emotion."

For several moments she was quiet, still, then her lips began to tremble, and her hands clenched and unclenched.

"There's nothing to fear," Cerviel said softly, gently. "You're just observing." When he saw her fingers relax, he smiled. "Excellent. Tell me what you see, Hallie? Are you alone?"

"No. I'm with my father." She sounded calm, even. "Out at our house on the lake in Minnesota. It's our favorite place to be." A smile touched her mouth. "It's summer, and we just got back from fishing. Me and Dad. We want to show her, my mom, what we caught. She always pretends to be scared of the fish, but she's not. She's not afraid of anything..."

"Hallie?" Cerviel whispered when she fell silent.

With the light from the lantern illuminating her face, he could see tension on her brow, her breathing increasing and her legs trembling.

"Hall—" But he was cut off.

"The door to the lake house is open," she whispered, pained. "I hear something... Oh, god, it's...Mom!" Her voice broke. "She's screaming. Dad and I...we drop everything, the fish, the tackle, everything and run inside—"

A cry escaped her lips and her face scrunched up in pain.

Shit. He had to get her back. *Now.*

"You're observing, Hallie," he reminded gently, moving in closer. "Listen to my voice. You're not there. You're here in the cave with me."

"They want me!" she cried, deaf to him now. "Oh god! They've come for me." Her eyes popped open, and they were huge and stunned as she stared at the ceiling of the cave. "It's my blood. From the transfusion I had when I was ten. I have the blood they want!"

Cerviel touched her arm. This had gone too far. He was going to bring her out.

But before he could say or do anything, Hallie was on him. With a snarl of fury, she shoved him to the ground and leaped on top of him. Cerviel's cat rushed to the edges of his skin, wanting to break free, but knowing it wasn't welcome outside the Wildlands. Straddling him, her face contorted in pain and anguish, Hallie reached out for his throat. A scream broke from her as she squeezed, her nails digging into the skin of his neck.

Even though his airway was threatened, he didn't touch her. Wouldn't dare. Her eyes were still open, but unfocused.

"Take me back!" she screamed. "Take me home! What are you doing? What are you doing to me?"

"Hallie," he whispered hoarsely. "Kitten, you're all right. You're safe."

"I'm going to kill you," she said through tightly gritted teeth, her fingers pressing deeper, harder into his flesh. "Just like you killed them." Her voice broke and her eyes filled with tears. "Made me watch... They were all I had. They were my life."

Fuck. Stars glittered before his eyes, but he didn't lay a hand on her. She was talking to whoever had abducted her. The bastards had murdered her family in front of her. No wonder she'd forgotten it all.

"Wake up, Hallie," he urged, his voice nearly gone from the pressure of her fingers. "Sweetheart. Look at me. Shit! Hallie!"

Her hands suddenly froze on his neck. She blinked. Then she started panting.

"You're here with me," he rasped. "Look at me, female."

Her eyes were darting right and left. She swallowed, blinked almost obsessively.

"Cerviel?" she hissed.

Her gaze dropped like a stone. To him. Her lips parted and she screamed.

"Oh my god, oh my god."

She ripped her hands from his neck and covered her own mouth with them. She stared down at him, at his neck, then up into his eyes. Tears were streaming down her cheeks, and she just kept shaking her head. Over and over.

"I'm so sorry." The words were muffled. "What have I done?"

"Hallie, it's okay."

"No! It's not." She scrambled off him and ran to the back of the cave. She wrapped her arms around her knees and sat there, rocking herself.

Shit. Goddess. He'd been wrong to press her on this. Clearly she hadn't been ready. What an asshole he was. Pushing her right after she'd come out of that hellhole.

He didn't go to her. For long minutes, he just sat there, saying nothing. Listening to the breeze outside the cave and letting her breathe—letting her come to terms with what she had revealed. What he'd forced her to reveal.

About ten minutes in, she finally spoke. Her voice was weary, but resolute. "I'm so sorry, Cerviel."

They weren't the words he wanted to hear. And he wasn't going to say it again, that she had nothing to be sorry for. She wouldn't hear it anyway. He wanted to know if she was okay, if her heart hurt, if she hated him for pushing her into the regression. But he suspected she wouldn't be truthful, vulnerable with him after what had happened.

So maybe he needed to be that for her.

"After Evie died," he said slowly, softly, "I woke up every night screaming for her. I thought she was still alive and when I learned she wasn't I tore my room apart. That went on for months. It always felt so real. It never gets perfect, Hallie, but I swear it gets better."

She didn't say anything.

"Did I fuck up, kitten?"

"No."

He shrugged. "I know the truth can be ugly as hell, but at least it's the truth, right?"

"I know. It's just…"

"Tell me."

"I didn't get a chance to mourn them," she whispered, tears in her voice. "Or miss them. Or say goodbye. I just—feel so...broken."

Yeah, I know. "Me too."

She inhaled sharply. "What do I do?"

He left his spot near the edge of the cave and went over to where she sat, her back to him, in the shadows of the lantern light. "You take time. As much as you need. And you heal." *I'll help you. Shit, I want to help.*

She turned around. "What if I don't ever heal? What if I can't forgive or forget? What if I can't live a normal life after everything that's happened?"

He stared at her, his heart thundering in his chest. Goddess, she was beautiful. All he wanted to do was take her pain away. He knew how she felt—well, some of it. Wanting to run, escape, anxious all the time... He reached out and brushed a tear-soaked strand of hair off her face, tucked it behind her ear. "Right now, all you have to do is breathe."

"What?"

He nodded. "In and out. One minute at a time. One hour at a time. One day... Don't worry about any of the rest of it."

They were so close, too close, their faces inches from one another. Her hazel eyes were almost green from her tears as she stared at him. Goddess, it was in direct violation of the blood oath he'd taken when joining the PSL—assets were off-limits—but he truly didn't give a shit. He wanted to taste her; her lips, her tongue, those tears. He wanted to hold her against him, stroke her hair and her back, take away her sadness and leave her with an everlasting smile.

And if it cost him his job, so be it.

As Raphael had said, sacrifices had to be made.

Maybe she felt it too, because as cold air rushed into the cave and swirled around them, she leaned in and brushed his lips with her own. Again.

"Hallie..." he ground out, his flesh tightening, his hands

balling into fists.

Instantly, she recoiled.

"What's wrong?" His cat was screaming for her, for more. For everything. "What are you doing?"

"You don't have to say it," she uttered, her eyes on the ground. "You don't have to say anything."

"What are you talking about?"

She crossed her arms over her chest protectively. "Look, I get it. You don't want to kiss me. I don't blame you. You've seen me at my worst. The lowest. I nearly choked you. And how I must've looked in that cage—" Her voice broke. "Naked and pathetic and used up—"

"Stop," he growled at her, taking her by the shoulders. "Right now." He knew his voice was as fierce as his gaze, but the moment demanded it. "Don't you ever speak of yourself like that again, do you hear me?"

Her eyes pricked with tears. "God, I'm such a fucking mess."

"No, Hallie. You are beautiful and kind and funny and real."

A sob wrenched from her throat.

The sound was a cannon in his soul and he crumbled. "I want to touch you, female. More than you can ever imagine. I ache with the need. Look at me. My face, my body. I'm tense, hungry, and my cock is more than ready." He released her arms and she sagged against him, her head to his chest. He groaned. It felt like fucking heaven. "I know I said it before, but it's true. You deserve more. You deserve time and space and—"

"Now you stop!" she shouted. She pointed at her chest. "Like *I* said before, Cerviel, I get to say what I motherfucking deserve!"

He stilled. "Of course you do. I just—"

"And I deserve this—you." She eased back and looked at him, her eyes searching his. "I've never been kissed until you. I've never been touched by anyone I desired until you. I've never felt pleasure and happiness under a male's hand. Only pain and humiliation." She reached up and curled her hand around the back of his neck. "Do I have to beg, Cerviel? Do I?" Her eyes implored him. "Because I will."

Beg? Goddess, was she serious with such a word? To just look upon her was an honor. To touch her... *Fuck...* He was humbled at the very thought.

"You never have to beg me for anything, kitten," he whispered, dropping his head and nuzzling her lips. "Never."

* * *

His kisses made her lightheaded.

Warm, wet, gentle, yet with an undercurrent of fierce hunger. He was going slow, for her. But she egged him on, coaxing him, letting him know she liked his ferocity. That it didn't make her cower in fear. In fact, fear had no place in her heart anymore. Not with this male at her side. He had not only given her the truth, stunning as it was, but he'd plucked her out of her nightmare and granted her a soft place to fall.

Groaning at the wondrous sensation, she drove her fingers into his thick hair and gripped his scalp. A soft snarl tore from his throat as she pressed him closer, tighter against her mouth. It was the strangest feeling. She couldn't seem to get enough of him, kiss him deeply enough, bite at his lower lip hard enough.

And then his hands stole around her waist and the pads of his fingers dragged up her back.

Oh, whoever, or whatever, is emerging inside of me, I say yes, yes, yes to it.

Ripping her mouth from his, she descended on his throat, kissing his skin and dragging her teeth over the bands of muscle she found there. She was going on instinct. She had so much to learn, but she was ready for it. For his touch, his mouth, his eyes on hers as his fingers explored every soft, wet inch of her. What had been done to her in that iron prison had nothing to do with intimacy. It had been all about violence and control. This was the complete opposite in every way. She was giving herself to this male. Freely, gladly, excitedly. Wanting more than anything to know what it felt like to need and desire another, instead of turning herself off like a switch, and enduring.

His hands held her tightly, safely as he eased back a few inches. Just so he could look at her. His eyes were so soft, as though he was looking at something precious.

You, Hallie. He's looking at you.

She shivered with the realization.

"I want to make you feel good, kitten. Happy, safe." He raised a brow. "You guide me, okay? Tell me to stop, slow down, speed up. I'm here for you."

Her heart tripped, then melted. Those words were priceless and so wonderfully exposed. And when he took her mouth again, and gently reclined her back on the smooth rock floor of the cave, she felt herself open completely. To him, to the moment, to a future that could be bright and happy and hopeful, if she embraced it.

A soft growl vibrated in his throat as he changed the angle of the kiss and lapped at her tongue with his own. The gesture instantly sent curls of tension spiraling through her body and she arched her back, wanting more, wanting to get closer. Impatience drove her a little mad, and she grabbed his hand and guided it down and under her sweatshirt. *Oh...*the feel of strong, safe hands on her sensitive skin.

"Talk to me, Hallie," he uttered against her lips, his voice like hot ash.

"Touch me. I want to feel you on my skin." *I want to feel you everywhere. I want you to claim every inch of me. Give me new memories, wonderful memories...*

She grabbed his wrist over the fabric and drew his hand up until he palmed her naked breast.

His sharp intake of breath against her mouth made her melt, made her turn liquid. Made her nipples harden.

"Oh, kitten," he whispered, his large hand squeezing her flesh, massaging, then easing back and teasing the tight bud between his thumb and forefinger.

A cry erupted from Hallie. She'd never felt such intensity, such rabid hunger. It almost scared her. Would it ever be enough? Would every touch, every kiss only fuel the flame that would rage inside her for this male?

"I don't know how much more I can take," Cerviel whispered, his fingers tantalizing her other breast now. "You are...something incomprehensible to me."

Hallie pulled him closer, kissed him hard and hungry as he squeezed and rolled her nipple. Her belly felt unbelievably tight and her sex was contracting in anticipation. It wanted him too, inside, deep inside...

"What is it like, Cerviel?" she asked breathlessly between hungry, demanding kisses.

"What, kitten?" he rasped.

"To shift into a puma?"

She could feel him smile against her lips. "Wild, intense, free."

"Like this?"

He pulled back a few inches. His eyes were wild and close to black. "Oh, *ma chère*, very close to this."

Every inch of skin on her body trembled with awareness and need. She sat up, forcing him off her for a moment. Without a word or a thought, she grabbed the hem of her sweatshirt and yanked it off.

"Kitten," he whispered, his voice a grave warning. "What are you doing?"

Toeing off her boots, she then quickly removed her pants and tossed them aside.

Her gaze went to him as she reclined back on the bed of leaves once again. "I've been like this for five years. In a strange way, I'm more comfortable naked than clothed. But I've never felt safe." She gave him a smile. "Until now. I've never wanted anyone to touch me." She reached for his hand and placed it on her stomach. "Until now."

She saw him visibly shudder with unbridled hunger. His eyes were polished stones and the muscles in his gorgeous face were contracting, pulsing. He looked like he was barely holding on, like he wanted to attack and graze and savor, but was afraid of such force and passion.

"You are so beautiful," he said, his gaze trained on her face, her eyes. "It's there, Hallie."

"What?"

"Your cat. I see her in your eyes."

Hallie guided his hand down until the tips of his fingers threaded into the hair covering her sex. "What does she look like now?"

His nostrils flared. "Fearsome."

She grinned.

He moved over her and his head dipped, his mouth closing over her nipple. Shards of exquisite pain lanced her pussy and she released a groan. His tongue was magic and talented, hot lashes and teasing bites. Her eyes closed and her hips canted and she commanded him to give her more, more, endlessly more.

"Oh, such soft fur you have, kitten." His fingers slipped between the lips of her sex, and when he found her slick, he snarled against her wet bud.

She shivered and thrust her hips up, higher, mindless. "Is it always like this?" she whispered breathlessly. "Like you want to crawl into each other's skin? Like you want to cry and laugh with each touch…each kiss? Like you don't want to come, but yet you do…so desperately."

"With the right one, it can be all of those things and more." He lifted his head and gazed down at her. His eyes glowed with a savage fire. "I believe."

Her breath hitched as he started to circle her clit. "You don't know?"

He shook his head, slowly. "But I think I'm beginning to."

She smiled, her heart clenching with a need to know everything about this male. How had he been sent to her? The One? Her One.

Don't do that. Don't claim him when you don't know how he feels, what he wants, what's coming.

"I want to feel inside you, Hallie," he said, slipping his fingers from her clit and moving them down. "How wet you are. How tight. You have to guide me."

She nodded. "But first…"

"Yes? Anything."

Her grin widened. "Shirt. Off."

His brow lifted.

"I want to feel your skin too."

A slow smile touched his beautiful mouth. "Done."

In seconds, he had his shirt and jacket off and his hands back where they belonged. Hallie held her breath waiting for the sweet invasion. And when he slid two fingers inside her, slow and deep, she gasped with unbridled pleasure. *This.* This was how it was supposed to feel. This was intimacy. Two beings wanting each other, connecting, making each other happy.

She never wanted it to end.

Cerviel found her mouth again and as he pumped her slowly, teasing her clit with his thumb, he kissed her. It wasn't savage or hungry, though she loved when he kissed her that way. No, he took his time, sucking her lower lip into his mouth, playing with her tongue, gently feeding from her as he thrust. And she touched him, explored the hot skin of his chest and waves upon waves of muscle.

It was strange. An amazing brand of strange. She no longer knew where she was, only that she was under the spell of this male. She saw only his hair and his forehead as she blinked. She was given over to him—not by anyone else, but by herself.

It was as if she was meant for him. In an ancient way.

"Oh, Cerviel," she suddenly gasped. He had stopped thrusting, but his fingers remained deep inside her. And he was doing something—something glorious, something that was making her insides quake and quicken. His fingertips were pressing on something... "It's..." she began. "The pressure, it's building, and the heat... I feel like I might go mad. It's supposed to feel like this, right?"

He raised his head and stared down at her. "Hallie... Oh, my beautiful kitten, you've never come before?"

Tears pricked her eyes. Is that what was happening? Her heart broke and she shook her head. "I wouldn't. I couldn't. No one was going to have that, steal that from me. It belongs to me." For a second she felt a thread of embarrassment move over her, but when his mouth covered hers once again, and he started to thrust into her with deep, wonderful strokes, she forgot everything but the total, consuming happiness and madness and emotional intensity that rose up in great waves inside her.

"Take it, Hallie," he whispered in between kisses. "Just as you said, it belongs to you. I'm honored I can be here, watching you. My beautiful female. Mine..."

The madness reached for her and grabbed hold. She cried out into the dark coolness of the cave, bucking against his hand, claiming each delicious wave of climax.

Mine.

Mine.

Finally mine.

Cerviel was watching her, his eyes on her face as he followed the movement of her body, his fingers sliding in and out, so wet. She rode him, again and again, chasing the incredible sensation. Until it receded and she lay there, in his strong, safe arms, spent.

Exhaustion unlike anything she'd ever known attempted to claim her, pull her under. But it wasn't fair. She wanted Cerviel... Wanted to touch him, taste him, make him growl out her name when he came…

"I want you," she whispered, nuzzling into him, her eyes unable to remain open. *I wish I could.*

"I have everything I need, everything I want right here." He pulled her close and kissed the top of her head. "Sleep, my kitten. We have plenty of time. You're with me now. Nothing will harm you. Ever again. Sleep easy tonight."

She couldn't argue with him. Her mind was lost and her body was replete. And his words were like a warm blanket over her heart, and to her bruised and battered psyche.

She gave in to his lulling, loving words and to the ache that had never left her in five years. To be able to sleep in peace and security.

Because in Cerviel's arms, she found both.

She'd found everything.

CHAPTER 7

Cerviel woke slowly and painfully.

He was hard as a hammer and his cat was clawing to get at the warm, soft female sleeping beside him.

Not that he was going to do anything about it. Dawn was coming. Though it was still dark, he could scent its approach in the air. And at first light, they needed to get the hell out of the cave and travel through some rugged terrain to reach the chopper.

He turned his head and glanced at the sleeping beauty wrapped in his arms. The light of the lantern was low now, but it gave off enough of a glow to see wild red hair, a gorgeous and very relaxed face and a good five feet of naked, pink skin. A few of those inches being her thigh, which was draped across his jean-clad shaft.

Torture.

He turned back and stared at the ceiling of the cave. *Repeat after me: getting her to safety is more important than rolling her to her back and slipping inside her.*

Or suckling her sweet nipples while he made her cry out again. Just the thought had his dick pulsing.

Down, you rabid motherfucker.

A soft buzzing sound at his side stole his attention. He'd removed his cell from his back pocket the night before and placed it right next to his side, along with his gun. Without waking Hallie, he grabbed it. *Shit. A text from Zagan.* What was he doing?

Where the fuck are you, C?

Delayed.

Delayed or getting laid?

What's the problem, Z?

The big boss is sending me to L.A.

Shit. Sry.

You know I can't go back there.

No choice.

We always have a choice.

Not if you want to stay a ghost.

Looks like I'm going to be resur-fucking-rected in L.A.

Steer clear of her.

Impossible. I'll be able to smell her the second I cross the border into Cali.

Beside him, Hallie stirred. He glanced at her and his chest tightened. *Gotta go, Z. Stay safe.*

Yeah. U too.

Slipping the phone back onto the rocks, Cerviel turned to the beautiful female who was making him consider the oath he'd taken, the rules he'd broken last night—remaining a ghost. How was he going to manage it? Having her and having the PSL?

Because sure as shit he wasn't giving up either.

Resisting the urge to climb on top of her and lick his way down her body until he reached the cream his cat wanted so badly to taste, he gave her shoulders a gentle squeeze. But instead of waking, stretching, she sighed and clung to him even tighter.

He ground his teeth. If his dick got any harder the thing was going to fall off.

"Kitten," he whispered in a measured yet gravelly tone.

She snuggled into his neck.

"We should go." His voice was anything but calm, cool. Every inch of him was sending out shock waves. The vibration had to be felt miles away, it was so intense. This female was going to be his addiction. One he couldn't and wouldn't shake. He could feel it. And if she woke up, she was going to feel it too. Pressing insistently against her thigh.

"Hallie…" he warned.

"No," she said on a very feminine groan, grinding her sex against the outside of his hipbone. "Not yet."

His eyes were going to roll into the back of his motherfucking head any second. "We don't have much time."

"How long?" she asked, lapping at his neck with her hot tongue.

He sucked air between his teeth and clenched his hands into fists. "Half hour max."

"Perfect," she whispered, kissing his neck, biting as she slid her hand down his chest and into the waistband of his jeans. "I can make that work." He could feel her smile against his skin as she took his cock in her hand and squeezed. "I can definitely make that work."

* * *

After the most perfect night of sleep, warm from this male's body, safe because of this male's promise, all Hallie wanted was to feel him on top of her, beneath her, against her…

Inside her.

So deep there would be no question to whom she belonged.

Maybe she was crazy to feel the way she did. Aching. Desperate to be completely taken and consumed by this male after five years of imprisonment and being forced…

No. Why did she even have to question herself? Her motives? For taking what she wanted? Asking for what she wanted? She deserved everything good and real. That heinous part of her life was over. She was the boss now. She took and gave because *she* wanted to. Because the brokenness inside her was slowly starting to repair with every kiss she gave and every smile he offered.

As she had the thought, her lips curved into a smile of her own. *Mine. You're mine, male,* she mused as she squeezed Cerviel's shaft. He felt like hot, smooth steel in her hand, and her insides hummed with a want she was just barely starting to understanding.

"You're unleashing a beast with that," Cerviel uttered on a growl.

Her smile widened. "Oh, I hope so." She couldn't even fully grip him, he was so thick. But she could stroke him. Up and down, squeezing him tight, brushing her thumb over the tip, following and reveling in his groans of pleasure.

The cave was still bathed in darkness, though a strange, steely light was starting to creep inside, comingling with the fading light of the lantern. But it was enough to see him, watch the bands of muscle in his neck tighten and pulse with strain, watch his finely chiseled stomach tense with every ragged breath.

But it wasn't enough to see…everything.

Releasing him momentarily, she grabbed the waist of his jeans and pulled them down to his ankles, then stripped them off completely. He wasn't wearing underwear, and for a just a moment she gazed at him. Beautiful, majestic, predatory.

Mine, she thought again as she crawled on top of him and

straddled his hips.

Cerviel's eyes widened and turned black with lust. And directly before her parted sex, his cock stood stiff and proud.

"Hallie," he said, his voice threaded with barely contained desire. "If I lift you up and place you down on my shaft... If I'm inside you, so deep you can't breathe, so deep I can't think...you will belong to me."

Her nipples tightened to buds, aching, desperate to be touched, and her pussy creamed against the shaft of his cock.

"Do you understand what I'm saying?" he urged, his face a mask of unbridled tension. "I'm Pantera, a puma. I can't possibly walk away from you after I've had you. I know that as I know my own name."

The thing...inside her was growling, clawing at the edges of her skin. It wanted to get to him. It wasn't to bite him.

"Please," he begged. "I'll let you go if I must. But push off me now...get dressed and wait outside—"

She didn't let him finish. She was up, on her knees and with her eyes pinned to his, she sat down forcefully on his cock.

A gasp ripped from her throat at the deep invasion, and for a moment—a delicious moment—she couldn't find air.

Cerviel let out a sound she'd never heard before in her life. Animal and male fused. And it did something to her. Caused a chemical reaction inside her. Her skin flushed, her breasts ached and inside her pussy, she felt anxious and wet. Very, very wet. And she had to move.

His hands closed around her hips and he started to rock her back and forward, every few seconds jacking up his hips to get himself deeper.

This was it, Hallie thought, her entire being humming with the music of this male's body and soul and heart and promise. This was how sex, making love, even fucking should feel. Utterly free, completely safe, and wonderfully connected.

"You're so tight, Hallie," he said through gritted teeth. "So warm. Your sweet pussy is sucking me deep."

Every word he uttered was like hot lightning exploding inside her body. Every thrust took her closer and closer to that amazing shatter of climax she'd experienced last night. But this time when she came her eyes would be on his—and they'd do it together.

"Cerviel," she cried as she circled her hips, grinding herself against him, her wet heat against his soft hair.

"Yes, *ma chère*. Tell me."

She shook her head and placed her hands on his chest, squeezing his pectoral muscles. "I just wanted to say it. Your name. On my tongue."

He growled at her and thrust into her over and over until she whimpered. Then he dragged his hands from her hips to her ass. "Come here. Let me have that tongue."

She was close, so close and if he kissed her, deep and hungry, she would fall over the edge and crash. But she followed his order—after all, he was her male—and leaned in, her hands bracketing his face.

"My kitten," he said near her lips. And with a light swat her to left ass cheek, he took her mouth in a deep, everlasting kiss.

Hallie smiled with sexual heat. "Tell me again, Cerviel. Tell me what happens after this."

He nipped at her lower lip, then swept her up in another hot kiss. "I can never let you go."

It was there, on the cliff. She just had to take it. She started to move, her hips lifting and lowering, rotating and grinding at a mad and fevered pace. Not only was she going to take what was hers, but she was going to send him there too.

"Never," he growled. "You're mine. Oh, fuck, kitten!"

Hallie's mind flashed red, then pink as she exploded. Her hands threaded in his hair and gripped his scalp. And as wave after wave crashed inside her, she held still, frozen, letting him take over, letting him pound into her as he too grabbed hold of the perfect bliss.

"Hallie," he snarled and growled as his body went mad and his fingers dug into her ass. "So hot! So fucking hot and soft..."

The cave echoed with the slap of their bodies and the cries of their release.

Cerviel didn't slow, not even as hot seed poured into her.

He was doing what a Pantera male did, she was certain of it. Something inside her understood and welcomed it.

He was marking her.

Good and deep and eternal.

CHAPTER 8

Dawn had broken, along with his vows as a member of the PSL.

But did he have one shred of a regret?

Fuck. No.

He'd deal with that when they returned.

Cerviel glanced over at the female he and his cat now called *MINE*. She was dressed, like him, but her hair was gloriously wild and free and her eyes still held the glow of her climax. They'd both dressed quickly, knowing the trek was long, and that the chopper would soon be arriving. But even so, Cerviel couldn't help himself. He went to her, took her hand and pulled her into his arms. The addiction. Wanting to feel her soft weight against him for as long as possible.

She released a sigh and let her head fall against his chest. They snuggled in silence for several minutes, then she tilted back her head to study him with a blatant curiosity.

"Why you?"

He gazed down at her beautiful face, trying to concentrate on her words when the only thing he wanted to do was kiss her, then remove her clothes again and lick her from head to toe.

"What?" he asked in absent tones.

"Why were you the one who came for me?"

He leaned in and kissed her nose. "You're not complaining, are you? It might break my heart, female."

A blush touched her cheeks. "I don't think you'd believe me if I did complain. Not after you made me melt into a puddle of goo last night and this morning."

He chuckled. He'd done his own share of melting. "Goo?" he teased.

She gave a firm nod. "Oh yeah."

Cerviel allowed the tips of his fingers to trail up and down the curve of her back. He smiled when a small shiver raced through her body. "Is goo good?"

She rolled her eyes. "So good. But stop fishing for compliments and answer my question," she commanded.

He paused. Usually he would have responded with a light quip that would have seemingly offered an explanation without telling her anything. He was a master at deflection and he could manipulate any conversation with an ease most politicians would envy.

But Hallie wasn't like everyone else.

She held a special place that was changing all the rules in his life.

Every second he was with her.

"I'm not really supposed to discuss the mission," he murmured, his loyalty to the league in conflict with his burgeoning loyalty to this female. He had to speak to Raphael. Once Hallie was recognized as his mate, things would be different. He would see to it.

She arched a brow. "Why not?"

"It's a secret," he told her.

Her lips twitched. "You have a secret identity?"

He gave a lift of one shoulder. "Actually, I do." He could practically feel the leader of the Pantera behind him, holding a noose—handing him his walking papers.

"Hmm." She laughed, clearly assuming that he was teasing her. "So what is it? CIA? Black ops?"

He exhaled. He'd never told anyone what he was about to reveal to her. "It's the PSL," he said. "The Pantera Security League."

She laughed again, enjoying what she assumed was a game.

"So you're a puma Jason Bourne?"

That quip he couldn't ignore. "With a better taste in clothes, I believe," he said.

Something in his expression made her still, the smile fading from her lips.

"This isn't a joke?"

"No," he assured her, wondering what she would think of his work. Granted, he would never be able to tell her everything, but he fully intended to give her what he could. "It's the truth, Hallie. Cerviel isn't even my real name, my birth name."

She eased away from him, studying him with a searching gaze. "What is it, then?"

He shook his head. "I can't even recall it. It's dead and buried. Each of us in the league took a new name. The name of an angel. Both light and dark." His brow lifted. "We thought it fitting."

Her eyes were wide and stunned as she took in what he was telling her. "Who was Cerviel?"

"He was a Principality angel." He felt his chin lifting as he explained, pride in the work he'd done over the many years. "He brought wisdom and encouragement to those facing challenges."

Her expression changed from shock to a soft understanding. "That does sound like you," she said with a gentle smile. "What does the league do?"

"Our leaders occasionally face decisions that aren't entirely black and white," he said, giving her a brief glimpse into his complicated life. "I work inside those gray areas."

Her lips parted, as if to demand a far more detailed explanation. But instead she lifted her hand to lightly touch his cheek. "Is it dangerous?"

Cerviel's heart missed a startled beat. He'd expected her to be curious, maybe even disturbed by the thought that he accepted duties that would make most people cringe. But at that moment, there was nothing but pure concern darkening her eyes.

"It can be," he slowly admitted.

She frowned, clearly troubled. Then, as her gaze searched his lean features, her lips twisted into a rueful smile. As if she'd caught something in his face that he barely recognized himself.

"You like it though, don't you?" she asked. "Putting yourself at risk?"

Yes. "I like helping those in need, and I like facing impossible odds and overcoming them," he said. He preferred to think of himself as a problem-solver rather than an adrenaline junkie. Far more dignified.

"Because it keeps you from remembering the past?" she pressed.

He grimaced. This whole "ability to see into his very soul" was going to take some getting used to.

It was true that he kept his mind occupied and his body in constant motion so he didn't have to deal with the lingering guilt.

But that wasn't the whole reason he remained a part of the league.

That he'd left everything and become a ghost.

"I want my life to have meaning," he told her. "More than ever after Evie died. Taking care of my pack, even if it's from the shadows, gives me the purpose I crave."

She nodded, her fingers tracing the line of his jaw. "Is that all you crave in your life?" she asked, her eyes taking on an entirely different glow of curiosity.

She was pretending. Acting as if his answer didn't matter. But Cerviel didn't miss the tentative yearning in her expression.

Nothing had ever mattered more.

"That's what I thought." He leaned in and brushed a soft kiss over her lips before lifting his head to hold her gaze. "Now, it seems, I have a new purpose."

He could feel Hallie's tension easing as he allowed his cat to glow in his eyes. As a male he could offer his heart, but his puma could offer his soul. An unbreakable bond that promised protection, devotion, and unwavering loyalty. *And Raphael will heed me.* It was time to revisit—or hell, rewrite—the rules on the PSL and mating.

Her fingers moved to trace his lips before she released a soft sigh. "How many are in the league besides you?"

"There are six of us," he said. *Leo. Nathanael. Ramiel. Zagan. Elyon.*

"Do they all have something to prove?" she asked.

Cerviel shrugged. He'd never truly thought about the glue that held the league together. Maybe they did have something to prove. To themselves. To someone else. He sure as shit had.

He did know that the reason they stayed was their loyalty to Raphael and the belief in his cause: protecting the species, the Pantera, at any cost.

"You'll be able to ask them in person," he assured, stealing one last kiss before reluctantly glancing toward the opening of the cave. It was still dark, but dawn would be arriving soon enough. "It's time."

She wrinkled her nose. "I figured."

"You ready?"

"As ready as I'll ever be," she said with a rueful sigh.

After making sure Hallie had her gun tucked into the pocket of her hoodie, he took her hand and headed toward the opening.

"Let's go."

Stepping out of the cave, Cerviel hesitated long enough draw in a deep breath. He caught the scent of rich pine needles, the crisp frost that coated the rocks in a slick shimmer of crystals. And a nearby den of chipmunks.

No indication that any humans had passed through the area.

Resisting the urge to keep her hand in his, Cerviel took the lead as they headed up the narrow pathway. There might not be the scent of humans, but that didn't mean there weren't any dangers ahead of them. He wanted to be prepared to fight if necessary.

They moved in silence, climbing over the boulders that blocked their path and weaving their way through the towering pine trees. At last they reached a trail that led over the ridge and down toward a shallow valley.

A pinkish glow was painting the edges of the sky as the trail widened and the forest thinned. The ground became treacherous as the loose dirt that was covered by tiny pebbles slipped beneath their feet.

Concentrating on his footing, Cerviel abruptly halted as the breeze stirred and he caught a familiar scent.

Two human males.

His nose wrinkled. Two *unwashed* human males. Did Donaldson's employees not understand basic hygiene? Or was the ex-congressman too cheap to offer them soap and water?

It wasn't the body odor, however, that made a growl rumble through his chest. It was the distinct metallic smell that warned the humans were heavily armed.

Glancing around, he sought a means to continue down the steep slope without using the main pathway.

"There," he at last murmured, pointing through the shadows toward a huge boulder that looked like it had been picked up and dropped by a giant to crack in two pieces. "Do you think you can squeeze through there?"

She gave a sharp nod. "Yes."

"Good. Head through and take the path to the bottom of the hill. The chopper should be arriving within fifteen or twenty minutes."

She frowned. "What about you?"

"There's at least one guard watching the trail. I'm going to provide a distraction."

She reached to grasp his arm, giving a shake of her head. "No, Cerviel."

He tossed her a quick smile. "Don't worry." He gently tugged free of her grasp, stepping back. This was what he did. Divert. Attack. Destroy. Simple as pie. "They can't catch me."

Her lips thinned. "Not even you can outrun a bullet."

A slow, smug smile curved his lips. "Don't bet on that, kitten," he warned, reaching out to give her a small push. "Go."

Her hands clenched, but she at last accepted that he would continue to put himself in danger until she was safely on the chopper. She sent him a glare that he assumed meant she was going to do bodily damage if he did anything stupid, then headed directly toward the boulder.

She moved with a silent elegance that revealed she had even more Pantera blood in her than he'd originally suspected.

Glorious female.

His female.

Waiting until she'd disappeared from view, Cerviel took a second to clear his thoughts, then with a lethal focus he melted into the lingering shadows.

There wasn't a sound to mark his passing. He might have been a ghost as he skimmed along the rim of the foothill, pausing as he reached the spot where the guards were stationed to keep watch on the trail.

Climbing onto a perch directly above the human, he studied his enemies.

The closest human male was thin, with long, greasy hair. He was clearly bored as he studied a spot on the sleeve of his too-large uniform. No doubt a token from his dinner the night before. The second male was much larger, with the bulk of a man who gained his muscles from steroids. He was staring into the distance as if he was a computer who'd powered down and was waiting for instructions.

Creepy as fuck.

Cerviel slowly straightened, allowing the first rays of dawn to outline his body.

He waited for the men to notice him. And waited. And waited.

With a roll of his eyes, Cerviel kicked a small rock, aiming it directly between the two men. As it clattered onto the ground, they at last glanced up. A momentary shock held them frozen in place.

Cerviel smiled, giving them a finger wave before he was leaping onto the back of the smaller man.

The human crumbled beneath the impact, smacking his head on a rock hard enough to knock him unconscious.

Cerviel kicked the limp body out of the way. He didn't want to trip over the idiot.

The larger guard grunted, grabbing his gun and squeezing off a wild shot. No surprise that it went wide. Cerviel doubted the man could hit the broad side of a barn even if he was aiming.

With a roundhouse kick, Cerviel knocked the weapon from the man's hand. Then, staking a spot on higher ground, he spread his legs wide. He waited for his opponent to either try and charge him, or flee in terror.

He wasn't disappointed when the man decided to charge.

Cerviel's hunger to destroy Donaldson extended to the bastards who wore his uniform.

Waiting for the man to take his first swing, Cerviel grabbed the massive fist. Crushing the man's fingers, he lifted his free arm to use his elbow to smash his nose.

The man shrieked like a howler monkey, backing away to cover his busted nose with his mangled fingers. "You son of a bitch," he whimpered.

Or at least that's what Cerviel thought he said. It was difficult to understand the words as his face began to swell.

Cerviel smiled. He could have toppled the guard backward with one shove. The bulk of his upper body not only impeded his ability to fight, but it made him top-heavy.

But what was the fun in that?

Instead he again aimed a kick at the man, connecting his heel squarely against his 'nads. There was a piercing screech. An octave above a high C. Cerviel took a second to appreciate his handiwork, then, strolling forward, he planted the tip of his finger between the man's crossed eyes to give him a small shove.

The guard fell backward, landing against the side of the hill.

Then, blessed gravity took over as the loose dirt beneath the man's heavy frame gave way.

Toppling head over heels he tumbled down the hill, picking up speed until he hit the bottom with shuddering force.

Cerviel peered over the edge.

The man lay spread-eagled, his head tilted to an odd angle as he stared blindly at the sky.

Satisfied, Cerviel stepped back. Time to head to the…

He abruptly stilled as he caught a familiar scent.

Donaldson.

Well, well. The man had gone to the trouble of personally climbing the mountain, just so Cerviel could kill him.

Pretty damned thoughtful of him.

Cerviel hissed in anticipation.

Time for a little fun.

Hurrying toward a pile of large rocks that created a natural barrier, he waited for the approaching male to round the tip of the rocks. Then, with a smooth motion he stepped forward.

"Hello, Donaldson."

The man jerked to a halt, his arm lifting to reveal the small silver pistol he held in his hand.

"Don't move," he commanded.

Cerviel smiled with a lethal anticipation.

The man looked like a toad with his short, squat body. Despite the chilled air a film of sweat glistened on the dome of his head, trickling into the fringe of hair that refused to concede defeat.

"I was afraid I might not get the opportunity to kill you with my bare hands," Cerviel drawled. "You've made it so much easier."

The pale gaze flickered over Cerviel's shoulder. "Where's the female?"

Cerviel shrugged. "Out of your reach."

Donaldson stretched his lips into what was supposed to be a sneer, but instead was just a weird contortion of his face.

"Come out, Hallie," he called out loudly, waving his gun. "Before I shoot your Prince Charming."

Cerviel stilled, afraid the dumbass might shoot him by accident. "I told you, you piece of rotting shit," he said, stepping forward as the man started to backtrack, "she's long gone."

"Don't move," Donaldson snapped, giving another wave of his gun.

Idiot. "Don't be ridiculous," Cerviel drawled, taking another step. "I can't rip out your throat from this distance."

More waving of the gun. "I'll shoot. I swear."

Cerviel laughed, glancing down at the pistol. "And you think that will hurt me?"

The man looked briefly confused. As if wondering whether or not Cerviel was crazy. Then realization hit him with enough force to make him gasp.

"Shit," he breathed. "You're a Pantera."

Cerviel pursed his lips, releasing a low whistle. "Well, well. You're smarter than you look." He flicked a gaze up and down the man's toadlike body. "Of course, that's not saying much," he conceded.

The broad face drained of color. Unfortunately, his fingers tightened on the gun. "I might not kill you, but I can disable you until my guards arrive," he blustered.

Cerviel came to a halt, and lifted a hand to cover a yawn. He'd always found the best way to deal with a bully was to refuse to react to their provocation. "Ah," he drawled. "About your guards."

The man licked his lips. "What about them?"

Cerviel used his thumb to gesture over his shoulder to where the first guard was still sprawled on the ground, blood leaking from his forehead.

"One is napping," he said, then jerked his thumb to the steep hill to their left. "And the other decided he preferred the view from the bottom of the mountain."

"Christ," the man hissed, his pallor replaced with an ugly flush of fury. "I suppose you really do get what you pay for."

Cerviel gave a lift of his hands. "And now it's just us," he said, closely monitoring the man in front of him. He wanted to see if Donaldson's gaze strayed to the rough terrain. That would indicate he had another guard lurking around.

When the man merely gave a disgusted shake of his head, Cerviel allowed his attention to focus squarely on Donaldson.

"What do you want?" the man demanded.

Cerviel heaved a disappointed sigh. "Weren't you listening? I told you I want you dead."

A twitch developed beneath the man's pig eyes as he forced a sharp laugh. "I don't believe that. Everyone wants something." He cleared his throat, taking an awkward step backward. "Money? I can put a hundred thousand dollars in your hand within the hour." More eye twitching as Cerviel gave a shake of his head. "Power? I can get you direct access to the congress. You can get whatever you want for your kind."

Cerviel snorted. He'd seen how the human politicians would promise everything to their people and deliver nothing.

"Once again, I told you what I want," he said, prowling forward. "Blood. Or more specifically, *your* blood."

Donaldson backpedaled even faster, his feet slipping on the loose pebbles. "I haven't done anything to you."

Cerviel closed the distance between them. "You used and abused a vulnerable female. You caged her. Humiliated her. Lied to her." There was a dark, lethal pause. "You raped her."

Sweat trickled down the man's broad face. "It was just a bit of fun."

Cerviel bared his teeth, allowing his cat to glow in his eyes. "Ah," he snarled. "Then maybe I'll take you home with me. We can keep you in cage and hire you out for a bit of fun. Would you like that? I know a few humans who'd enjoy hearing a pig like you squeal."

"Look, I only did what I was ordered to do." The man hastily tried to deflect the blame from himself.

Spineless coward.

"Ordered by who?" Cerviel demanded.

"Christopher Benson."

A low snarl was wrenched from Cerviel's lips. Christopher Benson had caused his people incalculable harm over the years. There wasn't a Pantera in the world who wasn't hoping to be the one to rip out the bastard's throat.

Cerviel sucked in a calming breath. He needed answers. Then he could punish Donaldson for every second of pain and humiliation Hallie had suffered.

"Why?" he asked.

Donaldson tried to look innocent. "He didn't tell me."

Cerviel allowed his gaze to skim down to the man's feet before returning to study the sweaty face. "Did you know pumas prefer to eat their dinner while it's still alive?" he asked. He snapped his teeth in Donaldson's direction, making the idiot jump in fear.

"Wait," he rasped, as if terrified Cerviel might start feeding on him at any second. "Benson didn't tell me anything, but I know there was something different about the female."

Cerviel stilled, barely daring to breathe. This was precisely the information they needed. "Different how?" he pressed.

The man swallowed heavily, his eyes darting around as if ensuring there was no one near who could overhear them.

"I think she was altered," he at last said, his voice husky with fear.

"Her blood." It wasn't a question.

"Yes, that too. But Benson once told me that he'd—"

There was a distant crack, like two rocks slamming together. It took a split second for Cerviel to recognize the sound. A split second too long.

Leaping forward he knocked Donaldson to the ground. But even as he landed on top of the spongy body, he could see the life leach from the man's eyes. What the fuck? He'd taken a bullet straight through the temple.

Cerviel scrambled toward a nearby boulder as a second crack echoed through the air. There was a blast of dust as the bullet buried itself in the rock.

Whoever was shooting was a pro.

Shit.

With a frustrated glance toward the dead Donaldson, Cerviel forced himself to leap onto the high ridge above him and disappear into a line of nearby trees.

Someone didn't want Donaldson talking to him about Hallie. But why? They'd already discovered that Benson Enterprises was capturing Pantera to use in their sick experiments. And that they'd infected humans with their blood.

What did they have to hide? What had he been about to reveal before that bullet ended him?

Keeping low to the ground, he pulled out the small device he had hidden in his pocket. He'd planted the bombs around the ranch house before ever entering it to find "the asset." He'd intended to wait until he was in the air before he blew the packs of high explosives, assuming that Donaldson and his friends would be deep asleep.

But now Donaldson was dead and he needed a distraction. He couldn't be sure that there wasn't a second hidden in shadows.

Pressing the button, he waited until the ground shook and a distant sound of destruction echoed through the air. *Ah. A sweet melody.*

Turning, he pocketed the device and headed for the helicopter he'd heard approaching during his fight with Donaldson. He hoped like hell that the men who'd intended to abuse Hallie had just exploded into a million itty-bitty bloody pieces. He didn't have time to hunt each one down and rip out their hearts, as much fun as that would be.

His future, both immediate and long-lasting, belonged to his mate.

CHAPTER 9

Sitting strapped into a seat in the back of the chopper, Hallie frantically pressed her face against the window. *Come on, come on, come on.*

Where was he? He was just supposed to create a distraction, then join her. How long could that take?

Clearly too long, as the pilot's voice popped and crackled through the headphones he'd insisted she wear.

"Time's up," he warned her.

"No."

With shaky hands, Hallie reached for the metal buckle that held the complicated seatbelt together. Then she slid forward and reached for the latch to the side door.

The pilot turned his head to glare at her with open annoyance. "What do you think you're doing?"

"I'm not leaving without Cerviel," she said, yanking on the latch that refused to budge.

Dammit, it had to be locked.

"Listen, lady, I have my orders," he snapped, reminding Hallie she was still wearing the headphones.

"I'm not a lady," she snapped back. *I'm a Pantera.*

"I'm on the ground ten minutes and then I take off," he continued, unfazed by her statement. "With or without passengers."

"Fine. Then you'll have to go without passengers," she informed him. "I'm getting off."

Without warning, the door slid open from the outside and Cerviel crawled into the cabin.

His nostrils flared and he quickly glanced at the pilot, then turned back to Hallie and gave her a wry look. "Trouble?"

With a choked cry, she threw herself against him, nearly tumbling back out of the chopper.

"Is she yours?" the pilot demanded with undisguised irritation.

Cerviel wrapped her tightly in his arms, pressing a kiss to the top of her head.

"Oh, yeah," he said, his heated musk wrapping around her. "She's mine."

The pilot snorted. "Good luck."

Scooping Hallie off her feet, Cerviel settled her in her seat. "Buckle up, kitten," he murmured, crouching in front of her to help with the straps.

Her heart beating wildly and so full she could hardly speak, she reached out to touch his face, realizing that she'd been terrified that something had happened to him.

Fate had been inexplicably cruel to her, but she'd lived through hell at the hands of Donaldson. Still, she knew that the agony she'd suffered in that cage and out would be nothing compared to the horror of losing this male.

Just the thought made her entire body tremble with a soul-deep relief.

"I wasn't leaving without you," she breathed.

He clicked the buckle, leaning forward to brush her lips in a kiss that was far too brief.

If it wasn't for the pilot, who was busily preparing for takeoff, she would have pushed Cerviel to his back and crawled on top of him. Staked her claim once again. She needed the heat of his body and the taste of his lips to assure her that he was truly here, alive and unharmed.

As if sensing her shattered reaction, he framed her face in his hands, kissing her with all the raw emotion that matched what churned inside her.

Endless time passed before he slowly lifted his head to study her with eyes that'd gone cat-gold.

"Don't worry," he assured her, speaking loud enough to be heard over the blades spinning above them. "Wherever you are, no matter how much distance is between us, I'll find you."

She held his gaze. "You promise?"

He didn't hesitate. "Oh, kitten, with my heart and soul. And you know that's true," he added with a wink as the pilot motioned for takeoff. "Because both of them belong to you."

CHAPTER 10

"Let me get this straight," Raphael said with a bite to his tone. "You want to change the terms of the contract?"

"There was no contract," Cerviel reminded him.

Under the warm bayou sun, the leader of the Pantera glared at him. "You shed your blood and your name and your life when you joined the PSL. You agreed to certain rules that would not only keep you hidden, but ensure the entire league remained safe."

The truth was only that. Truth. It meant nothing in the face of love. Yes, loyalty to The Six, to the Pantera, ran deep in his blood. But Hallie was the very air he breathed. He didn't want to choose between them, but if he was forced...

Standing outside the safe house, a cozy cottage built from weathered wood and surrounded by large weeping willows that made it impossible to see from the road—which was hidden several miles north of the Wildlands—Cerviel readied himself for another round of *Have you lost your fucking mind, ghost?* A few hours before, Raphael had met them at the private airstrip now owned by the Pantera, then had spent most of the drive to the Wildlands grilling Cerviel on every detail of his rescue of Hallie. Not to mention chastising him for the mating he'd allowed to happen.

As if mating was ever a choice.

When they'd finally reached the border, Cerviel wasn't surprised to find one of the Healers and a highly trusted Suit called Michel waiting for them. Raphael was convinced there was something different about Hallie that would make her a threat to Benson Enterprises and he wanted her fully checked over.

Cerviel didn't give a shit and had fought the leader over his proposed edicts.

All he wanted was to be alone with his mate.

Hallie, however, quickly proved that she was perfectly capable of making her own decisions. Ignoring Cerviel's protest, she allowed the young female Healer to do a thorough examination.

"Are you even listening to me, Cerviel?" Raphael demanded.

A rush of wind over the bayou moved over and through them. Nostrils flared, Cerviel took in the scent of pain and happiness, uncertainty and...*home*.

"You have a mate, Raphael," he said at long last.

The statement took Raphael by surprise, but he quickly recovered with a terse, "Ashe has nothing to do with this."

"Agreed." Cerviel leaned against the porch rail of the cottage. "I'm appealing to you, as a male. As a Pantera male." Crossing his arms over his chest, he asked plainly, "If you had been in my position, met your female as I met mine, would you have been able to walk away from her?"

Raphael's eyes flashed imperiously. "I didn't agree to the life you did, Cerviel."

"Would you have been able to walk away?" he pressed. "Under any circumstances?"

Raphael stood there, the Wildlands at his back, and said nothing.

He didn't have to.

Pushing away from the railing, Cerviel glanced back at the cottage, where his female now resided. Where they would both reside until the rest of the PSL brought in their assets. "All I'm asking, boss, is that you think about it."

"Think about what?" The scent of another Pantera rushed Cerviel's nostrils before the words were completely out of her mouth.

He turned, along with Raphael, to see Elyon walking toward them. Although with Ely, it was more like a strut. The fellow member of the Pantera Security League was dressed in her typical work gear: jeans, a white T-shirt and motorcycle jacket. Clearly, she'd just come from around the side of the cottage. How the hell hadn't either one of them heard her?

The female Diplomat was easily six foot and sleekly muscled. Her silver-white hair was buzzed close to her head, her skin was a soft caramel and her eyes were this crazy shade of blue with little streaks of jade in them. She was like a badass Barbie doll, and males completely lost their shit when she was around. Cerviel never got it though. Maybe because he saw her as family.

"Tell her, Cerviel," Raphael urged, a dark grin on his face. "See what one of your own has to say on the subject."

Ripping the Band-Aid off was always the best way to deal with Elyon. Even though she was inclined to pour a little acid on the wound afterward. "I took a mate." Simple. To the point. And no doubt, she would have a field day with it.

She flashed him a look of unbridled disdain. "Are you fucking kidding me?"

Raphael laughed.

"Didn't plan it, Ely, okay?" Cerviel told her. "Didn't go looking for it. You know me."

"I thought I did." She snorted. "Wait until Ram hears about this. You're going to be so screwed."

"Oh, shit," Raphael said, dragging a hand through his hair. "I forgot he had to walk away from his female to join the league."

"Well, he hasn't forgotten it," Ely ground out.

"Listen," Cerviel bit back. "Both of you." His eyes landed on each of them with unapologetic ferocity. "You want me out, I can't stop that. Do whatever you need to do. But Hallie's mine."

"Her name's Hallie?" Elyon snorted. Again.

"Yes, it is," Raphael said. "And technically, she's mine."

Cerviel's head snapped around. His eyes narrowed and he bared his teeth. He'd always prided himself on the fact that he had amazing self-control. But the leader's words had gone into his ear, and pierced the very heart of his cat.

As Elyon called out "Oh, shit" on a laugh, he leapt on the leader, knocked him to the ground and coiled over him, ready to shed some serious blood.

"Goddess," Raphael ground out, then flipped the male onto his back. "For now, Cerviel. Hear me before we both do some damage. She has a purpose here. She will stay until that purpose is revealed."

The male stood up and offered Cerviel a hand.

"Fine," he uttered, his voice dark and dusty as he grabbed the hand and came to his feet. "I will be staying with her though."

"Oh for fuck's sake."

Elyon laughed. "I can't do shit here, Raphael. But it was a nice thought."

"You called her in to reason with me?" Cerviel demanded. "Seriously?"

The leader shrugged. "I try anything and everything. The six of you are talented as hell, but you're all pains in my ass."

"Well, this pain is out of here," Elyon stated. "I'm wanted elsewhere. Try not to kill each other while I'm gone."

She took off back the way she came. And seconds later, the front door of the cottage opened and Michel walked out.

Cerviel was in the Suit's face the second his boot hit the ground. "Well?"

He glanced first at Raphael, then turned to Cerviel. "The Healer said there's evidence of the trauma she's suffered over the years, but there's nothing that won't eventually heal. She's given Hallie a clean bill of health."

Cerviel released a breath he hadn't even known he was holding. "Thank the Goddess."

Michel held up a slender hand. "But she did say that there was…" His words trailed away.

"What?" Both Raphael and Cerviel spoke at once.

Michel grimaced. "Something that she could sense, but

couldn't actually find. Like an echo of power hidden deep inside her, but dormant."

Cerviel scowled. "What the hell does that mean?"

"I don't know," Michel said.

"We will most definitely keep a close eye on her—" Raphael began, but Cerviel growled his disapproval.

"Oh, hell no. There's no 'we' keeping eyes on Hallie. Only me."

Raphael looked at Michel and heaved a resigned sigh. "The Goddess save me from newly mated males."

The Suit chuckled. "It's a problem we both know all too well."

Growing impatient to see Hallie, Cerviel snapped, "Is that all?"

The older male flicked a brow upward. "Are you trying to get rid of us?"

"Yeah," Cerviel said bluntly. "Clearly it isn't working very well."

As Michel laughed once again, Raphael growled softly. "Fine. For now. You can remain at the safe house together. But stay out of sight."

"You realize its me you're talking to, don't you?"

"I'm not sure who you are anymore." His eyes attempted to pierce a hole through Cerviel's skull.

Good luck with that. The thing is made of steel.

"If you notice anything, and I mean anything at all…unusual about Hallie, I want you to call me."

"Yeah, yeah. Go away."

Teeth gritted, Raphael gave a shake of his head, then motioned for Michel and headed back toward the border. Cerviel could hear scraps of their words—plans and concerns regarding the remaining assets—floating back to him on the breeze, but he didn't attempt to decipher more. Right now, he was only interested in one thing.

His mate.

* * *

Though they weren't exactly inside the Wildlands, the beauty, the air and the bayou near the border in the remote location in front of the safe house had an almost medicinal effect on Hallie. As she walked on the bank beside the slow-moving water with the male she now called her own, she felt at ease. She felt safe.

She felt at home.

But she wondered, couldn't help but wonder, as Cerviel's hand wrapped around hers, how he would feel crossing back over into a world that believed him dead.

If that was indeed the plan.

Things were so very much up in the air at the moment. The leader of the Pantera wished her to remain at the safe house indefinitely. For study. More questions. Perhaps even something dire. And Cerviel had refused to leave her. Goddess only knew what the future would bring. But at least they would face it together.

"Where are we going?" she asked him, so deep in thought she hadn't noticed they had gone farther into the bayou—the cottage no longer in sight.

"A favorite spot of mine."

"Oh, then I definitely want to see it."

He glanced over at her, his eyes chocolate in the warm sunlight. "Being here with you, it's changed things for me, Hallie. Everything feels new again, not tainted with pain and sadness. But open, I guess. To possibilities."

Her heart squeezed. "I'm so glad. When you walked down those stairs at the ranch, it changed everything for me." She stopped and turned, looked up at him. "You healed me, Cerviel. My heart, my soul, my outlook."

He pulled her into his arms, kissed her gently. "I'll never be apart from you. Or you from me."

She nodded, tears pricking her eyes. "Listen, I know we have to stay here for a little while, figure out what I know or have that's so vital to the Pantera, but if after that you want to go, leave the Wildlands behind and never come back, I'm with you."

Something flickered in his eyes. Raw emotion, perhaps even love… It was there inside her too, so she recognized it. Then he glanced past her, into the distance, toward the wild land of the Pantera and a wistful expression took over his features.

"I would love to take you there, my home. Used to be. I'd love to show you a real life, out of the shadows and into the light." His gaze returned to hers. It was soft and adoring. "The Wildlands has such beautiful light, kitten."

"Your parents…" she began tentatively.

He nodded. "Remember what I told you about facing your past, and the truth?"

"Sets you free?"

"Yes." He shrugged. "We'll just have to wait and see."

"I'm good with that. As long as I have you waiting right alongside me." She grinned up at him. "There are so many things we can do while we're waiting."

A low growl rumbled in his chest and his eyes darkened. "Agreed. And I say there's no time like the present." One dark eyebrow lifted seductively. "You know where we are right now, kitten?"

A ripple of excitement went through her. "Tell me."

"We're just shy of the border." His eyes glistened, and when he blinked, Hallie was sure she saw something feline behind his pupils.

The look sent her body into flames and she inched closer to him. She was all for making love on the soft patch of ground beneath their feet. Hell, with Cerviel, she was for it anywhere, anytime.

"The magic extends a few feet," he continued, his tone husky and deep. "You want to?"

The implication of his words sent jolts of electricity to all her warm, wet parts. She nodded eagerly.

But when he suddenly released her and backed up a foot, she was left confused, and irritatingly sexually frustrated.

Sensing or maybe scenting her mood, Cerviel chuckled. "Later, kitten. I promise. All day and all night. But first…"

She didn't understand. She stared at him. Waiting.

"There's magic where we stand," he said, then growled at her.

But it was no growl she'd ever heard from him before. There was no male in it. Only feline. It reminded her of her dreams.

Nerves gripped her as she now understood what he was asking. What he was attempting to bring forth. "What if I don't have it?" she muttered. "What if it's not there and you—"

"No more what ifs, kitten," he interrupted, his eyes fixed on her. "I know she's in you. Takes one to know one, *ma chère*." He grinned. "Now. Bring her on. Let her come out and play. With her mate."

Inside Hallie's body a potion was brewing. One she didn't seem to have to add to or even stir. It was just there. And this male, and this land—this magic—called to it and forced it to rise like a phoenix from the ashes.

Just as she had from that cage.

Eyes closed, she felt a rush of intense heat. It overtook her, every inch, including her mind. It was like a tornado. She was flipped and tossed about, then, all at once, everything halted. Almost painfully. She cried out, felt hands on her…skin?

Skin…

Fur…

Her eyes opened. She blinked against the brightness. Strange…so strange. How was it possible? Things looked larger, like the trees and the bayou. And she was low to the ground, but felt strong, invincible.

Amazing.

Cerviel was grinning from ear to ear. "I knew it," he said, excitement in his voice as his gaze moved over her. "You're gorgeous, kitten. Auburn coat, and eyes so green they put emeralds to shame."

Hallie opened her mouth to speak, but only snarls and hisses came forth. A slight thread of panic erupted in her. This would take some getting used to.

She looked around, stalked forward, feeling the warm ground beneath her feet. No, not feet. *Paws.*

She felt on edge, hungry, but not for food. For movement. The air on her muzzle. Scents in the air rushing her...

"I know," Cerviel said with a smile that lit her world. "I know what you need. I need it too."

Unlike her, Cerviel shifted in seconds. It was a fast rush in a strange mist and there he was. He stalked over to her and rubbed his head against her, lapped at her ear with his tongue. And she purred. Goddess have mercy, in cat form, she truly felt everything times ten. A heightened awareness. A driving hunger.

An almost manic desire when her eyes took in the massive golden puma before her, with his fierce gold eyes.

He snarled at her. An invitation to play. And she crouched, low. For a brief moment, he seemed confused. Then, like a switch being hit, he got it. She was giving him a head start.

Cerviel took off down the bank, and seconds later, Hallie's puma followed, racing after him. The wind in her fur, the scents in her nose. And her love...her puma, her mate, her protector, her savior, leading her into a brand new and glorious world.

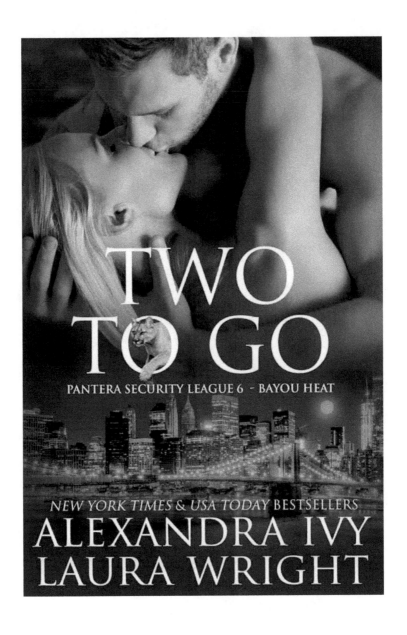

TWO TO GO

PANTERA SECURITY LEAGUE 6 - BAYOU HEAT

NEW YORK TIMES & USA TODAY BESTSELLERS

ALEXANDRA IVY
LAURA WRIGHT

TWO TO GO

PANTERA SECURITY LEAGUE 6 - BAYOU HEAT

ALEXANDRA IVY
LAURA WRIGHT

CHAPTER 1

She was a ghost.

Didn't exist.

It was part of the deal.

The shit they'd each signed. Not with a pen or in blood or anything, but with their agreement to join the Pantera Security League. While *some* weren't taking that agreement very seriously—*Cough, cough, Cerviel!*—she did. With every breath she drew into her lungs.

The safe house at her back, the sun overhead, Elyon picked up speed, racing through the wetlands, darting in and out of the cypress. She never ventured into the Wildlands, of course. *Rules, bitches, remember?* But she did get…close. Close enough to work her favorite magic.

Shifting into her cat.

Shifting out of her cat.

Back and forth, like a blink of the eye, clicks on a camera. The feeling was a total rush. Heat and cold, wet and dry, hunger, then thirst. It was such an infrequent luxury to have fur on her back, and with each mile she covered, her frustration, her irritation at her fellow Six member started to ease. Unfortunately it couldn't cease altogether, because that would be impossible. After all, the male had just declared some crazy shit back there. Calling someone his. Unwilling to leave her side. Declaring her his mate.

Hallie. That was her name.

Cue the eyeroll.

Elyon shifted into her cat again and snarled at a bird trying to keep pace with her. She couldn't believe Cerviel had stepped over that line.

And with an asset!

She flashed back into her female form just as a rush of wind hit her face. Maybe she should give Ramiel a head's up in L.A. so he didn't completely lose his shit when he found out. Go hunting for Cerviel. Or Raphael. It was, after all, the big boss who'd told her fellow ghost to end it with that female who was *this close* to becoming his mate. Made him choose.

And now he was letting C off the hook like that...

Not cool.

After she'd completed her mission, she'd make a quickie trip to Hollyweird, take the male for a drink, or seven, and spill the beans. Unless, by some miracle, Cerviel had come to his senses and cut things off with *Hallie* by then—or at the very least he'd have something to say for himself that didn't include long stretches of silence while he stared at the asset, drool running down his chin.

She leapt over a fallen log, shifting into her puma midflight. *Yeah, baby.* Not that she was opposed to drool. Or guys, males, drooling. When it was aimed at her, of course. She was, after all, a six foot, sleekly muscled hottie with silver-white hair that she'd buzzed close to her head. Her smooth skin was the color of caramel and her eyes were a brilliant, passionate blue. She'd had men drooling from the day she'd grown breasts. Once upon a time it had been a curse. Now it was just plain fun.

But she'd never, ever—*ever*—give up her life, her work, her vow for a Drooler.

Mating was a true sucker's bet.

And love? She laughed. Didn't exist. Not in her past, present, or future.

A scent hit her cat's nostrils and she hissed into the wind. She was close. Almost there...

The thing was, she didn't begrudge Cerviel or any of the males she worked with a little piece on the side—some action when they needed it. She was known to take what she wanted when she wanted it too. Maybe it wasn't even the mating that bothered her so much. But witnessing her friend so openly vulnerable. He had trust in his eyes…love, belief that *Hallie* was worth giving up everything for. Trusting her with his very soul. He didn't know what that meant. What damage could be done.

She did.

And no matter what, she'd make certain that no one ever came close to touching her soul on such a primal level.

She'd eat their heart if they tried.

Her cat leaped onto the bank in front of the abandoned one-room shack. For several seconds, she allowed it to frolic in the water, kicking up mud and plants. It wasn't until her entire coat glistened in the sun that she shook herself off, then shifted back into her jeans and leather.

"Can't stay away from this place, can you, Ely?"

The leader of the Suits had shifted midstride and was walking toward her with a grin. The top brass of the Diplomatic faction of the Pantera was pure, golden perfection. Thick blond hair, richly tanned skin, and eyes that were jade at the moment, but glowed with liquid amber power in his cat form.

"Hey, boss," she called out as he approached. "This little shit shack was my home at one point. And we always come home, don't we?"

"Only if we have information to share with the class," he replied.

As the male's scent settled around her like a cloak, Elyon's cat purred. Raphael was one of very few in the world she considered a part of her pack. Along with The Six, of course. Not that she fully trusted him—that honor went to no one but herself—but she believed in him. Looked up to him. Respected him. And was eternally grateful to him.

After all, he'd saved her.

Unlike most Pantera, she hadn't been raised in the Wildlands. Her parents had been Diplomats, working in Central America.

Passing as wealthy human business owners, they'd been targeted by a local gang. Their house had been ransacked, but they'd only taken one thing. The most precious item her parents possessed.

Her.

Like the true cowards they were, the men had snatched Elyon when she was in the care of the housekeeper, and soon after a ransom was demanded for her return. She'd only been five freaking years old, but it had taken the men less than a day to realize there was something different about her. *Poor babies. Not!* Scared by her stunning strength and eyes that glowed blue fire, they panicked. Instead of dropping her on the doorstep of her terrified parents, they'd taken her to the jungle and dumped her in a swift-moving river. No doubt they'd hoped she'd drown, her body swept away by the water. Or perhaps eaten by one of the numerous predators.

Too bad, asshats. Death was so not her. She'd not only survived, she'd thrived.

Became a predator herself.

Granted, she hadn't been able to shift into her puma form, being outside the magic of the Wildlands, but she had the instincts of a wild animal. A few months later she'd been found and taken in by two ancient sisters who lived together in a village that was way, way off the grid. They'd cared for her, loved her in their way, and treated her like their own cub.

Not at all surprisingly, the memories of her real family grew distant and indistinct pretty damn quick. That is, until Raphael walked into the village and claimed her as a Pantera. How he'd found her he wouldn't reveal. But he'd insisted she return to the Wildlands. At least long enough to allow her puma to be given the opportunity to be released. Bless him for that. It had been glorious. But, unfortunately, once there, she'd sort of freaked out, emotionally. She'd refused his pleas for her to be reunited with her parents. Thing was, she just hadn't been ready to open herself up to her family. Two Pantera she barely remembered. Not yet.

So, Raphael had given her an option.

To become a part of the Pantera Security League. Or "The Six," as they called themselves. To become Elyon, the angel who guided, comforted, and protected, but who also brought plagues on the houses of anyone who tried to screw with her. And truly, she'd never regretted saying yes to that offer.

Even when the news of her parents' death had come to her eight months after her return. Goddess on high, she'd actually been grateful. The work had stolen every dark thought, every great and powerful wave of guilt, every deep regret, and turned it into supreme productivity.

And an iron wall around her heart.

"You have something to share, Ely?" Raphael said, his gaze constantly moving, always aware of his surroundings.

When Pantera were away from the Wildlands, even a hair over the border, they were always looking for trouble.

Especially these days.

She nodded. "I do. I managed to locate the 'RR' that was on the message."

Interest sparked in the older male's eyes. Just a week before, Xavier, the head of the Geeks, had intercepted a message from their enemy, Christopher Benson.

"Code red. Dispose of all test subjects at Rattlesnake Ranch, China House, The Orchard, Mulberry Lane, Battle Creek, and RR."

Cerviel had just returned with the test subject at Rattlesnake Ranch. *Hallie. The Mate.* Now it was Elyon's turn. Though her asset retrieval was going to go a helluva lot differently. Get in, locate, extract, deliver.

"Tell me," Raphael commanded.

She glanced around the remote area and the safe house she'd spent many months at when she'd come home with Raphael. There didn't seem to be anything to concern herself with, but life had taught her to be cautious. She always assumed that there was someone hiding in the shadows, or listening from the bushes.

Paranoia? Maybe. But it'd kept her alive.

"I was able to run the names you found in the original message against the files we managed to download from Benson Enterprises," she told Raphael, turning back to face him.

She was nothing if not resourceful. From online to inside. When she'd first started up with the PSL, she'd discovered that she might not have her parents' skill as a Diplomat, but she did possess an uncanny ability to blend into the criminal subculture. She felt perfectly at home with human predators. Thieves, cutthroats, dealers... And she could blend in easily despite her Amazonian size. The general population couldn't tell at a glance that she was Pantera, but they could sense the danger that smoldered around her with an unspoken warning that a person with a half a brain didn't want to screw with her.

"You got a hit?" Raphael pressed.

She nodded. "RR. Russian Room."

Not surprisingly, the leader scowled. "What is it?"

She reached into the pocket of her leather coat, pulling out her phone. With a few swipes of her finger she found the image she was searching for. A narrow brick building with a large front window and an iron door. It was three stories, with old-fashioned fire escape ladders zigzagging between the barred windows and a flat roof. She held it up to show him.

"On the surface it's a small restaurant in New York City," she explained.

Raphael leaned forward, studying the image. "And beneath the surface?"

"Underground fight club."

He released his breath with a low hiss of fury. "They're using Pantera to fight?"

"That was my first thought too," Elyon said, feeling her cat scratching at her insides. Poor furry girl. Wanted out again. One taste was never enough. For either of them. "But I don't think that's what's going on. I've done some heavy-duty research on the place and it looks like the typical hangout for overly aggressive humans who feel the need to pound the crap out of each other." Sounded like a show not to missed. If only she had the time.

Raphael nodded, trusting her words without question. That was what she appreciated most about him. He gave her a task and then trusted her to complete it. No looking over her shoulder, or pestering her with micromanagement.

"What's the connection to Benson?" he instead asked.

"His corporation owns the building," she said. It'd taken her hours to unravel the complicated tax forms that'd at finally led back to Christopher Benson. But she was nothing if not persistent. And an insomniac.

"What's their interest in a human fight club?" Raphael spoke his thoughts out loud.

"I'm on my way to find out."

"You're taking this one?" Raphael demanded.

"Unless you have an issue with it," she said, then gave him no time to argue. "I've already prepped my backstory and uploaded it to the usual sites used by fighters." A smug smile curved her lips. She might be a Suit by birth, but her hacking skills were pretty damned impressive. Even if she did say so herself. "Come on, it's perfect for me. If anyone looks me up, I'm the Angel of Death who is just returning from Hong Kong." She patted the pocket of her coat. "I also asked for an old friend to email me an introduction."

Raphael arched a brow. "Do I know this friend?"

"Only if you happen to be a part of the Serbian mafia."

His lips twitched. He knew better than to ask how she became acquainted with a man who ran Serbia's crime syndicate.

Hey, she knew a lot of people. Most of them unsavory characters who lived in the shadows of life, and who most upright—or uptight—citizens tried to avoid. But, no judgment.

"How are you getting there?" he asked as a warm breeze blew across the bayou.

She inhaled the familiar scents and *almost* wished she had an hour or two to just kick it by the water's edge. "I have a private flight booked for this afternoon."

He studied her for a long, silent moment. "Do you want me to have Leo go with you?"

Her brows snapped together. "Are you trying to piss me off?"

He stepped toward her, the power of his cat filling the air with sizzling heat. "We don't have enough intel to know what you're walking into."

She slammed her fists on her hips, her own cat sliding near the surface as she glared at her mentor. No longer did it want to come out and play. The furry bitch inside her wanted blood. Seriously. If it'd been anyone but Raphael questioning her solo abilities, she would have made them regret even voicing the question.

"I can handle it," she said through tightly gritted teeth.

Raphael made a sound of impatience. "I know that, Elyon. But it's not always bad to have a partner."

She stepped back. It was her natural reaction to anyone who tried to invade her personal space. Whether it was physical or mental.

No. Trespassing. Period.

Even with Raph.

"I prefer to work alone."

Raphael released a soft, resigned sigh. "Yeah. That's what scares me."

Understanding dawned. This partner thing wasn't about capability to him. It was about vulnerability. "I think you're going soft in your old age."

He wasn't baited. "Call it whatever you want."

"Okay. I'm calling it a pain in my ass. You're not my father, Raphael."

"No, but I hope I'm your friend."

Damn him. He was always doing this kind of shit to her. His kind, truthful words making her flinch. Making her belly go kind soft. Okay, fine. She knew she could be difficult.

She was aloof. Aggressive. And prickly.

A genuine bitch.

But she deeply valued the few people she allowed past her barriers. Like The Six. And this awesome leader of the Pantera. The male who'd found her, freed her.

"Of course you are," she said, chewing her lip. "Course you're a friend." *Jeez.*

He folded his arms over his chest, giving a faint shake of his head. "When I asked you to be a part of the Pantera Security League, I hoped that it would give your life a sense of purpose."

"It has."

He acted as if he didn't hear her. "But I didn't count on the fact that your work would isolate you even more."

"I'm not isolated," she protested. And she wasn't. She spent most of her time in big cities, trolling the streets for information that couldn't be found by more formal techniques. It was amazing what she could learn, shit that was just floating along in the sewers of humanity.

Raphael wasn't fooled by her flippant response.

"Oh yeah? When was the last time you spent more than an hour or two with your friends?" he challenged. "Or taken a lover?"

She sucked in a harsh breath, holding up her hand. "Cerviel's bullshit has rubbed off on you. Clearly."

"I'm deadly serious."

"So am I. And grossed out. You might want to check yourself." Okay, so maybe he was kind of a father figure, after all.

"This isn't about mating," he pressed. "This is about connection. With anyone or anything."

"Okay, this conversation is over."

Raphael ignored the prickle of warning in the air. Typical. "Because you don't like the questions," he bit back.

"No, Raphael," she said tightly and pointedly. "Because who I do or don't have in my bed is none of your damned business."

He stared at her, eyes narrowed, silent as the grave. Waiting for more. Waiting for her to cave.

"Christ." Elyon spun on her heel and started away, from the water, safe house, and him. "I'm out of here. I have explosives to prep, and an asset to retrieve."

"Be careful, Elyon," Raphael called after her. "I'm here if you need me."

Please. She didn't need anyone. Not that she was going to turn around and tell him that because weapons prep was a helluva lot more interesting than standing around defending her capabilities or chitchatting about *connection* or who she was or wasn't boning.

As she moved farther away from the border, and her overly concerned mentor, her cat snarled with caged frustration inside her chest.

CHAPTER 2

Brewing coffee.

Steaming garbage.

Sizzling meat.

New York City, baby. Elyon grinned as she moved down the street, her long legs eating up the stained pavement. It was just after seven o'clock. Darkness had fallen over the Lower East Side, but the lights from the various bars and restaurants spilled out onto the sidewalk.

Dressed in a black leather jacket that hit her at the waist, skintight spandex pants, and heavy shitkickers, Elyon ignored the lingering stares from both men and women. She was single-minded now, utterly focused. Turning into a narrow alleyway, and only pausing long enough to stuff her small backpack into a dumpster. A bag that contained a hotel key card and enough explosives to take out the nearby brick building.

She grinned. She was definitely a female who liked to be prepared.

And hey, if she couldn't get her target? Same rules apply. She'd be forced to turn the place to rubble.

Not to mention, destroy anyone inside.

Once satisfied the bag was hidden beneath a layer of trash, she circled back to the front door and headed inside the restaurant. Instantly she was assaulted by the smell of meat, onions, and roasted beets. In the center of the dimly lit space there were a half dozen tables, all occupied by older men and women, large plates of stroganoff or bowls of borscht spread out before them. Immigrants who occasionally sought a taste of home? she wondered. Or paid shills who kept both an eye out and shit looking real.

She sniffed. Maybe a mixture of both.

She'd see soon enough, if anyone tried to stop her from…exploring further.

Her gaze searched the shabby interior, finally landing on a black curtain in the far back, opposite the kitchen. Feeling the eyes of the patrons clinging to her, she headed straight for it, ready to answer any questions with her fists, or her knees, or her foot. Her smile widened as she pushed past the curtain. The right one had been known to break multiple bones.

And the occasional boner.

But surprisingly, no one stopped her. Behind the black fabric, she found a narrow hallway, lit with the same god-awful florescent crap you'd find in an elementary school. Moving with a lazy grace, she crossed the cracked linoleum floor and turned right into another hallway that led to a narrow flight of stairs going up. The smells of food receded and were instantly replaced by the scents of a gym. Rubber mats, disinfectant, and sweat.

Bingo.

The lighting sucked the farther away from the restaurant she went. Only a bare lightbulb that did a piss-poor job of battling the thick shadows. Something that might have been dangerous if she didn't have her cat senses. As it was, she could easily see the man approaching her through the gloom.

As if his heavy steps and rank stench of vodka hadn't warned her first.

The stranger was a large beast. He had at least six inches on her, which was saying something, with powerful, broad shoulders. His dark hair was cropped into a military flat-top and his features were bluntly cut, with pale eyes.

He was wearing a pair of camo pants and a white ribbed tank top, and he had that expression that said, *I'm either going to kill you or eat you.*

Poser.

And so boringly predictable.

She headed for the stairs, already prepared for Mr. Meathead to get in her face or grab her arm.

"Hang on, sweetheart," he growled, doing both. "Where do you think you're going?"

She arched a brow, then glanced down at the thick fingers that circled her arm. Another asshole thinking it was okay to get in a female's personal space. As she glanced back up, making a *tsk tsk* sound with her tongue and teeth, she noticed a second human male. This one had come out of a door to the left and was climbing down the stairs.

"One. Two," she counted slowly, her gaze returning to the hand on her arm.

"Did you hear me?" the man snapped.

Elyon grinned. She'd have to be deaf not to hear this asshole's grunts.

Her nostrils flared and she let the scents wash over her. "Three. Four." She continued her counting.

"Bitch, you'd better get your hot ass out of here or I'm going to—"

"Five." She interrupted his flattering yet unwelcome threat, moving with blinding speed.

The man released a shrill scream as Elyon wrapped her fingers around his wrist, squeezing hard enough to shatter his bones. *Pretty.*

She didn't stop there.

Still holding his mangled wrist, she whirled to the side. The motion dragged him off his feet and slammed his body against the brick wall. There was a loud thud. Like a sandbag hitting cement. A very large, very sweaty sandbag.

She released her hold, a taunting smile curving her lips as the man gave a groggy shake of his head and forced himself to his feet.

"I did count," she said in sweet tones.

The guard swore in Serbian, then charged forward. Elyon

heaved an uninterested sigh, neatly stepping out of the way. Really, it was sad. There was a time when the Russian mafia hired only the best fighters. Now it seemed their standards had gone straight into the gutter.

Who the hell charged in such a narrow space?

Waiting until he was lumbering past her, Elyon swirled to lift her leg. She kicked him in the ass, sending him shooting into the brick wall on the other side of the hall. This time the sound was more of a crack than a thud as his skull connected with the bricks.

He groaned, sliding to the floor with a dazed expression.

"Nice move." A male voice sliced through the air, his accent hinting to a childhood spent in Moscow. "Can I help you with something?"

With a last glance to ensure the guard wasn't intending any surprise attacks, Elyon turned her attention to the man who was standing on the lowest step.

He was short and square with thick salt-and-pepper hair that was greased back from his florid face. He had heavy jowls and dark-rimmed glasses that were tinted to hide his eyes. An old trick that was supposed to intimidate opponents back in the day.

He looked like the stereotypical Russian mob boss.

Seriously, the entire place was just one big cliché, she silently, and irritatingly, concluded.

"That depends," she told him.

"On what?"

"On how much money you can offer me."

He shrugged, raising his hand to study his manicured nails. "You know how to cook stroganoff? Or are you a waitress?" he asked, pretending not to know why she was there.

Heh heh. Idiot.

"I'm asking how big your purse is," she bluntly demanded.

There was a gurgled sound from the guard who was trying to raise his bloody head.

"Grr?" Elyon released a sharp laugh, nudging his ribs with the toe of her boot. "Is that Serbian for 'I just got my ass kicked by a girl'?"

The man on the stairs clicked his tongue. "Clearly I need to upgrade my security."

"You're Victor Sokolov?"

The man glanced toward the opening that led to the restaurant. The sound of muted conversations drifted through the air. Along with a new scent that made her stomach rumble. Meat and vinegar. She'd really hate having to blow this place up before she got a plate of whatever that was.

"In my office," he abruptly commanded.

Victor turned to climb the steps with surprising speed.

Yes, sir. Grinning, Elyon followed behind him, taking the stairs three at a time. Once they reached the top, she had a brief glimpse around an open space that had been converted into a gym with a large boxing ring in the center of a wood-planked floor. There was the typical weightlifting equipment, an area with several punching bags, and a treadmill.

There were also three separate doors that were closed.

The man in front of her opened the closest one, and stepped inside. She paused, allowing her senses to sweep the confined space to ensure there was nothing lurking inside.

It was empty.

Still, she waited until he'd moved across the cramped space to lean against the desk littered with messy piles of papers before she stepped over the threshold.

"Look, *milaya*—" the older man started.

"Name's Elyon," she interrupted, her expression hard with warning.

No one was allowed to call her honey or darling or sweetie or babe. In any language.

Not unless they wanted their face rearranged.

"Fine, Elyon," he conceded in patronizing tones. "I appreciate your..." He deliberately paused. "Balls, but I run the best club in town. Which means I don't let every stray fighter who walks through the door in the ring. Even if they're smoking hot. It's invitation only."

She reached into the pocket of her coat, removing the email she'd printed out before leaving for New York.

"Consider this my invitation," she said, holding it out.

The man grabbed the paper and swiftly scanned the brief note. His brows climbed up his forehead. If this man considered himself the best in New York, then he had to know that Karl Richardt was the best in the world.

"You know Richardt?" he breathed.

"I've fought in his tournaments."

The man tossed the paper on the desk and pulled out a phone from the inner pocket of his tailored suit. He was smart enough not to accept a possibly fake email as proof of her credentials.

Bravo.

He texted someone, hopefully Richardt, who owed her big time for that ex-lover issue she'd helped him solve, then typed her name into a search engine and pulled up the bogus information she'd uploaded.

"The Angel of Death, eh?" he read out loud.

She hid her smile at the ridiculous name she'd given herself. Cage match fighters were all about the drama. And hey, she was an angel to her PSL family. At least when she wasn't being a hellish pain in the ass.

"When can I be added to the roster?" she asked.

His phone pinged and he glanced at it before returning it to his pocket, his expression now satisfied that she was who she was pretending to be.

"It's not that simple," he told her.

She rolled her eyes. "It never is."

He shrugged. "If you aren't a part of the local circuit then you have to fight our club champion before you can be included on the roster."

"Fine." She placed her hands on her hips, her foot tapping with impatience. "I'm ready. Anytime."

The man considered her for a long minute, clearly calculating how best he could take advantage of her. His gaze skimmed up and down her tight, muscular form, lingering on her buzzed hair and the lean features that were more striking than beautiful.

He had to know that she would bring in large crowds if she could actually fight.

"Tonight," he abruptly announced.

She gave a sharp nod. *Hot damn.* It was exactly what she'd been hoping for. "I need to see the facilities."

He frowned. "Why"

"I don't come into a fight blind," she told him, her stubborn expression telling Victor she wasn't going to take no for an answer. "I want to walk the space and get a feel for the actual ring."

Victor shrugged, pushing away from the desk to head out of the office.

"Follow me," he ordered, crossing toward the center of the gym. "Max," he called out.

Across the vast space, a door opened, revealing what looked like a locker room. A male stepped out wearing nothing more than a loose pair of basketball shorts. Even his feet were bare.

He closed the door behind himself and started forward. At them. At her. Elyon hissed out whatever was left of the air inside her lungs, feeling like she'd just taken a sucker punch.

And maybe she had.

Holy shit.

She'd never seen such a stunning example of male hotness in her life.

Her gaze moved languidly up his body. Like a tongue lapping at an ice cream cone. He was six foot six of pure muscle. His shoulders were broad, his chest thick, and his massive legs were long and perfectly formed. He had a thick black braid that swung down his back and a boldly handsome face with chiseled features. His eyes were an icy amber color rimmed with gold.

As he neared, Elyon could see dark markings across his chest. Not the usual "I'm the shit" tats that one normally saw on humans. Nope, these were dramatic angel wings that spread from his heart and over his pecs. They were exquisite, but Elyon didn't miss the white blemishes beneath.

This man had been tortured.

This male, she corrected.

And it'd happened before he'd been given the Pantera blood that she could smell running through his veins. Otherwise, he would never have scarred.

"Meet our club champion," Victor drawled. "Max. The Hammer."

The Hammer, huh? Suited him. Suited him real well.

Elyon forced an indifferent expression onto her face even as she felt the world tilt beneath her feet.

He was a hot, ripped warrior with eyes that would no doubt stay open and fierce as he fucked his female. She was all over that. But it wasn't what was making her legs tremble, her breasts tighten, and her very soul shatter as she stared at him.

A moment ago, she was the same Elyon she'd been from her earliest memory. Strong. Wary. Class-A bitch. And now, she was completely undone and remade into a new, unfamiliar female.

Breathless.

Vulnerable.

Scared out of her freaking mind.

Ashamed.

And it was all because of this male.

Her *mate.*

The word came too quickly and easily from her insides. Impossible. Impossible. Impossible. She fought back against them. Punch, kick, stab, blow up! She was no one's mate. Ever.

Attracted—that's what was going on. Like, seriously wanting

to jump this male's formidable bones and maybe come up for air a week later.

Like, crazy insane lust.

Shaking her head for a second, she allowed her gaze to roam over him again. Up and down, then back up again. Every solid inch. Accepting the lust. But, that wasn't it. Wasn't all.

Oh, shit... He was trouble with a capital T, bold and in italics! And she was insane, off her game, ready to be committed. Good-fucking-Goddess! How could she accept the feelings rushing through her? She wasn't that female.

Hell. No.

But no matter what her brain conjured as far as reality, refusal and impossibility—her blood, and the cat beneath her skin begged to differ. It screamed and raged that this was it, this was the one. It clawed at her ribs, and panted from the delicious wonder of it.

It was always the way. With everything. When the female on the outside tried to ignore the facts, the cat inside just...knew.

Fuck. Me.

This guy. This male... He couldn't be the one, if there was ever really going to be a one, which she'd formally sworn that there wasn't. He was her asset. She was on a mission.

Her shoulders slumped. Of all the gin joints in all the towns in all the world...

The words from "Casablanca," her favorite flick, whispered through the back of her mind before she was grimly shutting down the inane thoughts once again.

And again.

She was going to have to wash her mind out with acid. But later. After retrieval or possible explosions. Right now, she needed to catch her breath, kill her lust, and focus.

"And this," Victor was speaking, waving a hand toward Elyon, "is the Angel of Death."

"Elyon," she firmly insisted, giving a nod of her head toward the male.

He returned the nod, his aquiline nose flaring. She watched him. Did he detect the musk of her cat? Was he capable? His eyes dilated before he was doing his own share of hiding his expression. Oh, yeah, he definitely felt something.

Welcome to the club, honey.

"Max," he said, his voice a low rumble in his chest.

Victor stepped back. "Show her around."

The male's brows snapped together. "She's here to fight?"

Uh oh...boyfriend doesn't like that.

Ely rolled her eyes at her stray thought. Her dangerous, dangerous, idiotic thought.

Victor pointed a stubby finger in Max's direction. "Just do as you're told."

Max clenched his hands into tight fists. "Whatever," he muttered, watching as Victor turned and headed out of the gym and down the stairs.

Studying his air of resigned and very sexy petulance, Elyon wasn't prepared when the massive male abruptly whirled around and grabbed her by the shoulders. The next thing she knew her back was pressed against the wall and Max was nose to nose with her, his gaze searing like fire over her face.

Her eyes widened in surprise.

God. Damn.

Gimme more, boyfriend.

She blinked, her heart pounding in her chest, her belly clenching. Why wasn't she fighting back? And more importantly, why wasn't her issue with personal space being triggered?

Oh, yeah.

T.R.O.U.B.L.E.

***

Max glared at the woman who'd set off all sorts of alarm bells the minute he'd set eyes on her.

Christ, she was a magnificent creature.

A tall, brutal work of art. Like a pureblood racehorse. Or a sleek, predatory cat.

Elegant lines. Supple power. A sexual challenge that made something inside him roar with hunger.

It was no wonder he was achingly hard.

But it wasn't her stunning looks that was sending tiny jolts of fear through him. Nope. It was the unmistakable scent that teased at his nose and made the primal part of him snarl with recognition.

It was a scent that he thought he'd put behind him when he'd left the cages in New Orleans to be put in a different cage here in New York.

"Who are you?" he snarled softly at her.

She lifted her hands, placing them against his chest and giving him a shove. "Back off," she snapped.

It took far more effort than it should have to keep himself from tumbling backward.

"Wrong answer," he replied, spreading his legs to keep his balance. "Who. Are. You?"

She narrowed her gaze, something lurking in the back of her glowing eyes. "Victor told you." The words slid off her lovely tongue so easily. "I'm the Angel of Death."

The name did suit her. And if she'd been a normal competitor, then he might have anticipated watching her fight. Maybe even climbing into one of the cages with her.

He sensed, however, she was anything but normal. And that there was a specific reason she was standing in the gym, eyeing him as if he...

Well, he wasn't sure how she'd be eyeing him, but this, what she was doing right now, felt intimate as fuck. Possessive.

Irresistible.

His dick pulsed.

"You aren't human," he ground out, his tone accusing.

She snapped her teeth, nearly taking off the tip of his nose.

"Neither are you."

With a scowl he glanced toward the camera set in the ceiling above them. The gym was constantly monitored, but the cameras only transmitted video. The guards wouldn't be able to hear them speak.

Releasing his hold on her, he stepped back and motioned around the gym. "Let's walk."

He turned and started to stroll around the boxing ring in the center of the floor, pointing toward the heavy weightlifting equipment. She hesitantly fell into step beside him, her brow furrowed until she at last realized he was performing for the cameras.

She gave a faint nod, pausing to pretend to study the nearest treadmill.

He kept his gaze locked on the control panel, even as he stepped to the side, until his shoulder brushed hers. Electric awareness zapped through him at the light touch.

As if he'd just been seared with a cattle prod.

The hot zap was a sensation that had happened more than once in his life. Although it was never a pleasant one.

This, however… This felt fucking…

Spectacular.

"Who are you?" he demanded again, his voice low despite the fact the cameras wouldn't pick up his words. There was always an off chance someone was lurking on the stairs, or in Victor's office.

"I told you," she said, her eyes pinned to his.

The deep color slayed him. A real knock-me-out blue.

"Tell me again," he pressed, brow lifting. "Maybe this time you'll drop the truth."

"My name is Elyon."

The word, the name, hummed inside his skull. *Elyon.* Unusual. Exotic.

It fit her to perfection.

"*What* are you?" he continued.

She smiled, a real wicked twitch of the lips. "Pantera."

He wasn't surprised by her answer. He'd already suspected the truth. "Puma shifter," he breathed.

"Do you know about us?"

"Not everything. But enough." His hands clenched as memories jackhammered through him. The cramped cell. The sterile lab where he was strapped to a narrow gurney. The agonizing pain as the serum was pumped into his veins. "I was infected with your blood."

"*Infected?*" A low, dangerous growl rumbled in her throat. "Careful, Max. I might be here to rescue you, but that won't stop me from kicking your ass if you piss me off."

He dropped his head and touched the tip of his nose to hers. "You're welcome to try, Elyon. Oh, you're so welcome to try."

CHAPTER 3

Elyon tingled in places she'd never tingled before.

Hell, she didn't even know she *could* tingle in a few of those places.

With a sharp motion she stepped back, an awareness that was so acute it bordered on pain licking through her body.

This male.

This glorious, dangerous, mysterious male. He was turning her razor-sharp mind to mush.

Trouble.

And a serious problem.

His gaze flickered in the direction of the overhead cameras before he was waving a hand toward the ring in the center. She assumed it was for legitimate boxers who came to the gym for training. There was no doubt a separate room where the cages were kept for the illegal bouts.

"Keep walking," he murmured.

"I'm assuming that you weren't given a choice in receiving the *gift* of our blood?" she asked.

His lips curved into a humorless smile at her deliberate twist of words. "No. I wasn't given a choice."

They stopped at the edge of the ring. "Tell me what happened," she commanded.

His jaw hardened, his expression went wary. Apparently, Max was like her. Being vulnerable was off limits, and trust had to be earned.

"Why should I?" he demanded.

She turned so they were face to face, holding his guarded

gaze. "Because I've come to get you the hell out of here."

He made a sound of disbelief. "You?"

She allowed the power of her cat to glow in her eyes. There was no denying the male was gorgeous and practically irresistible, but he had an amazing talent to rub against her nerves.

Strange, considering she rarely had enough interest in other people to be annoyed by them.

What did that say about her reaction to Max? *Hmmm. And ugh.*

"Do you doubt my ability?" she challenged.

His eyes narrowed. "No, I doubt your motivation. Why would you want to help me?" he demanded. "And why now?"

She hesitated, considering her words. Her cat might instinctively feel a connection to this male, but her PSL side understood that he was still a stranger.

For all she knew, he might be a pawn of their enemies.

"We recently intercepted a message—"

"Who's we?" he interrupted.

"The Pantera. The leaders in our community. I'm going to continue now, all right?"

He made a go-right-ahead gesture with his hand. His large, powerful, scarred hand...

"The message mentioned this gym, and an order to dispose of all test subjects," she finally said. "I'm assuming that's you unless there's someone else here who might qualify as a test subject?"

Pain and rage darkened his eyes and he ground out, "Nope. I'm the only freak in the neighborhood."

She grimaced. He was arrogant and an insulting pain in the ass, but she didn't want him to think of himself as a freak. It hurt something deep inside her. Her guts and her heart...her heritage.

"Then I'm here for you," she told him.

"Again...why?" he asked, unrelenting.

You're my mate. Okay, that wasn't her. It was her cat speaking. She shoved the furry irritant back down where it belonged. Where it would remain. "The enemy of my enemy is my friend." She gave a casual lift of her shoulder. "Simple enough?"

He drew in a deep breath, his nostrils flaring. Was he searching her scent to determine the truth of her words? If so, that would be incredible. It was a talent that many mature Pantera possessed. Strange that a human who had their blood forced into his veins would have such an instinct.

"You consider Victor an enemy of the Pantera?" he asked.

"Not Victor. Benson Enterprises," she corrected. Her eyes widened when he released a furious hiss. "You recognize the name?"

"I should." His fists twitched, as if he was struggling not to smash them into something. "The bastards are the ones responsible for doing this to me."

She tilted her head to the side, studying him with an unwavering intensity. Every band of muscle, every inch of skin that wasn't covered. Every white scar under that magnificent tattoo. Her tongue twitched.

"What precisely is *this*?" she asked. "What did they do?"

His muscles clenched, the air around them heating with the force of his inner emotions. Elyon let the sensation wash over her, trying like hell not to shiver. For a long moment she feared he wouldn't answer, that she'd be forced to ask again. Then, without warning, he jerked his head toward the ring.

"Let's spar," he said.

Her left eyebrow drew up. Either he was avoiding the conversation or he wanted to have it elsewhere. Either way, she would get something out of him. "You sure about that?"

His eyes darkened and his mouth twitched with humor. "I'll go easy on you."

Oh. She snorted softly. "Okay."

She slipped off her jacket, revealing the tight spandex top underneath, the one that left her arms bare and hugged close to the soft swell of her breasts. Instantly the air was filled with the scent of male arousal. She grinned. Clearly Max liked what he was seeing. Elyon bent over, tugging off her boots with a slow, teasing motion that was completely unfamiliar to her. As if she was stripping to please her male.

Clearly, she liked doing this to him.

Liked the reaction.

What the flying fuck was wrong her?

Completely unnerved by her thoughts and her behavior, Elyon leaped onto the edge of the ring and swung over the elastic ropes that framed the canvas floor. There was a faint bounce beneath her feet as Max vaulted over the ropes too and landed lightly beside her.

They both stepped to the center and turned to face each other. Adversaries. Really sexually attracted adversaries.

"Tell me what they did," she commanded, lifting her fists to a position in front of her face. "And keep it short." *I'm on edge here. I need to fight.*

His eyes still smoldered with an unmistakable heat. "Do I look like a man who keeps anything short?"

Oh, she hoped not, she mused inanely. Her traitorous gaze drifted down to the huge bulge in his shorts. *What a disappointment that would be.*

She shot out her right hand in a quick jab. "Give it a try."

He easily avoided her fist. "When I was young my father ran this small auto shop not far from here. Nothing fancy, but he made a decent living. Allowed my mother to stay home and take care of me. Thing was, his mechanical skills were a lot better than his talent for gambling." He kicked out his foot, making a sweep toward her legs. "He managed to get into the kind of debt that usually finds you flat on your back with a toe tag."

Elyon leaped over his leg, kicking out with her foot. It was aimed at Max's rock-hard six-pack, but he dodged behind her with startling speed. Momentarily off balance, she barely avoided the blow aimed at the center of her back.

He was good. Really good.

Heat blasted through her body. *Ely want.*

It was rare for her to find someone capable of sparring with her where she didn't have to pull her punches. And it was exciting as hell. Had she met her match?

No.

Mate.

"I assume it didn't get him a toe tag?" she asked, spinning to face him, silently telling her cat to keep quiet and play nice. Her arm lifted just in time to block his uppercut.

His expression settled into grim lines.

"I was a big kid for my age, so the men who held my dad's account agreed to let me pay it off by working on the docks."

She knocked aside his fist, returning with a counterpunch that should have landed directly on his firm jaw. Instead he danced away with ease.

"Doing what?" she asked.

"Unloading their private yachts."

She frowned, briefly confused by his explanation. Unloading a yacht didn't seem particularly difficult. Why not just hire Max? Even if he was a kid?

Her distraction lasted less than a fraction of a second, but it was enough time for Max to strike. One moment she was frowning in confusion, and the next he was leaping forward.

Oof. *Goddammit!* The air was knocked from her lungs as his broad shoulder hit her mid-section. She flew backward, hit the mat. She was already preparing to jack to her feet and kick some ass. Payback time. A great plan. Except for the fact that a very large form was landing on top of her before she could even move a muscle.

She released a low snarl, telling herself that it was anger pulsing through her body. Or hardcore embarrassment.

No one mounted her. Not unless she wanted to be mounted.

Another time? Maybe. Probably. *Just not now.*

She glared up at the male who was staring down at her with a smug grin. He loved the fact he'd managed to gain the upper hand.

The aggravating ass.

"You're very good," he said.

"Tell me something I don't know."

"But distracted." His grin widened. "Want to tell me what's on your mind, Elyon?"

Refusing to give him even more reason to gloat, Elyon placed her hands against his chest, but made no effort to push him off. Despite her Amazonian build, he had her by over a hundred pounds. There was no way she could force him off.

The only thing she could do was wait it out, pretend she was precisely where she wanted to be. Flat on her back with Max planted on top of her.

"Were they using the yachts for smuggling?" she asked. The thought had hit her the precise moment she'd been flying through the air. Great time for a lightbulb moment.

"Yeah," he said, his smug expression becoming distracted as he gazed down at her.

It seemed she wasn't the only one being affected by the press of their bodies together.

"Why didn't you leave?" she demanded, wondering idiotically, as his sizable cock jutted up against her hipbone, what the full weight of him would feel like. Without the layer, thin as it may be, of clothes.

"I tried. My parents and I were approached by a guy who said he could help us escape." His eyes darkened dangerously. "He claimed they needed workers in New Orleans. That we could start over with fake identities that would allow us to bury our pasts and become new people, or some shit like that."

An unexpected pang of sympathy twisted Elyon's heart. He'd been royally screwed, and she better than anyone understood the feeling of having her world turned upside down, being thrust into an existence where she had to fight every day just to survive.

It was no surprise that Max and his family leapt at the promise of being given the opportunity to start over with a clean slate. Who wouldn't?

"It was Benson," she said. Not a question. She knew that shithead's tactics by now.

A low growl rumbled in Max's throat, the force of his anger sending a tangible blast of heat through the air.

Elyon pushed down the shock of lust that barreled through her. Every emotion he felt seemed to radiate from him. From his skin, his eyes, his lips. It was truly the sexiest thing ever.

"They loaded us into a van," he continued. "Drove us to New Orleans, just like they promised. But when we got there, some asshole wearing a mask opened the door and shot us with tranquilizer guns on the spot."

His face tightened with tension and…hate, and maybe shame? She couldn't tell for sure.

"I woke up locked in a cell that was at the back of some lab. Smelled like cleaning solution." He cursed to himself. "I'll never forget that smell." His eyes found hers and they were oddly vulnerable. "Every time I even get a whiff of it, I'm gone. Done for."

Unbidden, she lifted her hand and touched the side of his neck. Just held it there, in some strange attempt at comfort. Not that she had any clue what that felt like, but it seemed right, real. And he wasn't flinching or pulling away.

"Was there anyone else locked in the cell with you?"

He shook his head. "I was alone, although I could hear the other prisoners. At the time I didn't know what happened to my parents."

Yeah. That she understood as well. "What did they do to you? Benson's grunts."

"I was tortured. Plain and simple." The words were hard. Bleak. Emotionless. "Varied from day to day. Sometimes they used a whip on me. Other times a knife."

Jesus.

"Hardly felt it after a while. Then something changed in me and I started to crave it. Every kick, every slash."

Around them, the air was thick. With pain and desire and rage. Elyon's hand slid from his neck to his chest, the tips of her fingers moving over the exquisite lines of his tattoos. She hissed as she felt the rough edge of a thick scar.

"At the end, when I would give them nothing, not a word, not even a motherfucking whimper, they would pierce my chest with iron rings and hang me from them."

Her back to the mat, her eyes on him, her cat roaring and scratching at her skin with fury, Elyon knew, for the first time in her life, a deep and unwavering blood hunger for revenge. Forget the mind and what was left of his heart, torture like that didn't leave the cells. Oh, Goddess, she hoped very much she crossed paths with the bastards who'd tortured Max. They would learn her definition of torture. For a very, very long time.

Forcing on a mask of composure, she asked softly, "Why do you think they'd do that to you?"

He smiled, but his eyes remained shark-like. "They wanted to see how much damage my body could take after they'd given me a dose of your Pantera blood."

"Oh fucking hell," she uttered on a low breath. No wonder… No wonder he'd called the blood infusion an infection. That was being kind. Polite. Restrained. Pantera blood running through his veins should be an honor, a great gift. But to him it was a constant reminder of a living nightmare.

She had to help him. In more ways than just the rescue. There was no turning back now. He had Pantera blood coursing through him. He was one of them now. And maybe, hopefully, in time, he would learn to appreciate what the infusions could offer him.

He was staring at her, studying her. "What's going on in there?"

She shook her head. "I'm just…It's bullshit. I'm sorry."

"Don't," he breathed, his expression brittle. As if he was holding onto his composure by a thin thread. "Not here."

"What do you mean? Where—"

He cut off her words by dropping his head and kissing her.

Just like that.

Hot lips on her cool ones.

The rough stroke of his tongue against hers.

Magic exploding through her.

Holy shit. She groaned at the wonder of it and canted her hips, feeling the heavy, hard weight of his cock against her belly. Hunger raged through her and she almost felt like sobbing. Never in her life had she wanted something so desperately she'd be willing to kill for it.

"Someone's coming," he whispered against her mouth.

Suddenly, his weight disappeared as he surged to his feet. Elyon too was up, standing by his side in seconds.

Her body might be convulsing with lust, but her survival instincts were honed to a fine edge. She'd already caught the scent of approaching humans.

On full alert, she watched as the two men entered the gym. Both wore sweatpants with matching hoodies. One was in gray, the other in black. They had their heads shaved and the bulging muscles that came from steroids rather than nature.

Jaws tight and nipples tighter, Elyon grimaced. Tweedle-dumb and Tweedle-dumber.

As if to prove the steroids had exterminated any brain cells they might have been hiding beneath their thick skulls, the men sashayed over to the ring, eying Elyon with a blatant sexual threat.

Oh, brother.

"Well, lookie what we have here," the man in gray sweats drawled, grabbing his crotch.

Seriously, why do men do that?

It's just...creepy.

"We're closed," Max snapped.

The man in black sweats snorted. Silently Elyon renamed him Idiot One as he leered at her as if she might actually be interested in his sorry ass.

"I wondered what brought you to this shithole place," he drawled at Max, but his eyes were pinned to Ely's chest. "Now I know. Fringe benefits."

Idiot Two laughed like that was the funniest joke in the world.

Seriously, this was getting embarrassing.

"How about you share some of those benefits?" Idiot Two suggested.

Max stepped forward, his body bristling with danger. And the musk of a male who was about to strike. "She's mine."

Elyon felt a moment of swoony goodness. *His, huh?*

As her cat was purring in delight, Idiot One was ruining the moment, clicking his tongue, and flexing his muscles as if afraid Elyon had missed fully appreciating them.

"Now that's not nice," he taunted, wagging a thick finger. "I thought we were friends."

Max bared his teeth and seemed to grow even taller, if that was possible. Elyon arched a brow and just...admired him. *Yum, yum.* Did the male know just how Pantera he looked at the moment? Probably not. But it was hot as hell. Like the stuff of dreams.

Very wet ones.

Oh lordy, what was she going to do with herself? This was the asset, due back to Raphael ASAP—and she'd as good as marked him.

Cerviel was going to mock her ass for eternity, and Ram...well, he'd never forgive her.

"I don't have friends," Max warned.

"That's true." Idiot Two strolled closer. "But that doesn't mean you can't share."

Max just shook his head. "I'd really advise turning around and walking away."

Idiot One stepped up next to his friend. "You might be Victor's current pet, but you can't beat both of us."

Elyon was so done.

She'd watched men like this bully and terrify women her entire life. There were few things she enjoyed more than teaching them how to act like gentlemen. And…if she was going to admit it to herself, there was the annoying fact that they'd interrupted some lip and tongue action that she would've really liked to have explored further.

"You want a taste of me?" Elyon asked them in her sweetest voice.

Eyes widening, it was Idiot One's turn to share his version of the crotch grab thing. Really, she should just kill him for that alone.

"Oh, I'm going to have more than a taste, sweetheart," he drawled.

Elyon rolled her eyes before glancing toward Max. "They're mine," she told him. "It's just too good, you know?"

Max's lips parted, as if he intended to argue with her. Then, meeting her gaze, he held up his hands in defeat. "Mind if I watch?"

Her cat was close enough to the surface to make her eyes glow and her skin prickle with heat. Pure power raced through her. "Oh, I'd be disappointed if you didn't," she murmured right before she pounced.

CHAPTER 4

Max folded his arms over his chest. It was the only way to stop himself from reaching out to grab Elyon and wrap her in his arms protectively.

This was some crazy shit. He didn't understand himself, or the overwhelming urge he had to shield her from the two fighters. He'd never acted so possessive of a female in his entire life. Let alone one he'd just met.

But he was smart enough to know that she wasn't a female who would thank him for his efforts.

Hell, she'd probably rip off his nuts.

Which was, you know, sexy as fuck.

Releasing a slow breath, he watched riveted as Elyon glanced from one man to the other, silently determining which was the more aggressive.

He knew both of them. Steve Hayward and his cousin Larry. They were local street thugs who'd been hired by Victor to enter the matches and take a beating from an up-and-coming contender. Neither had much talent, and even less brains.

That didn't, however, keep them from being dangerous.

They were savage brawlers who weren't above fighting dirty.

He watched, as with a sudden smile of anticipation, the female his body was even now crying out for, took one leaping step forward and soared over the top rope of the ring.

Damn, girl.

His eyes focused on her first opponent. Poor Steve. The guy was seriously stupid enough to assume a female was no match for him. Which was why he stood there with his arms open, as if he was going to catch her, instead of what he should've been doing.

Like running for his life.

Max thought he heard Elyon chuckle as she flew through the air, kicking out her foot to slam her heel directly into the idiot's face. There was the crunching sound of cartilage being shattered, followed by a high-pitched scream of pain. Steve instantly tented his fingers over his bloody nose as he stumbled backward.

Without breaking a sweat, or a nail, Elyon landed lightly on the floor, her hands already raised as Idiot Number Two rushed forward and took a swing. She blocked a massive left hook, and feinted to the side. Larry followed, lurching off balance. Elyon swept out her foot, tripping him as he stumbled past.

Larry fell face-first on the floor, landing with a heavy thud. Elyon turned and flashed Max a wicked smile. Her face was flushed and her eyes nearly ate him up. White-hot pleasure, plus a weird sense of pride, jolted through him.

He'd growled the word *Mine* at the two dickheads getting their obituaries written right now. But had he meant...that? Exactly that? How could he? He'd just met her, spilled his guts to her...this Pantera female who'd been sent to rescue him...

His gaze moved over her. Sleek, sexy, badass. Her attention had returned to Steve, who was shaking off her initial blow. Smart girl. First rule of fighting was to always know where the opponents were. And what state they were in.

With a bellow of anger, Steve put his head down and charged forward, looking like an enraged bull. Elyon shook her head, as if she couldn't believe he was that stupid.

Waiting until he was almost on top of her, she used her cat-reflexes to jump straight upward. At the same time, she aimed her knee directly at the man's swollen nose.

Thud. Crash.

Exquisite. The shot and the girl.

Steve's head jerked backward, blood flying from his nose. Max grimaced. The man might never breathe through that thing again.

Dropping to his knees, Steve cradled his head in his arms, clearly trying to protect himself from another blow.

"Seriously?" Elyon mocked, her voice filled with disapproval. "You whine like a baby."

There was a muttered curse from Larry as he hauled himself to his feet.

"Think you're tough, bitch?" he snapped.

Max thought about being pissed for the verbal cut the asshole had sent her way, but truly he felt more pity for the guy. He was about to get axed. Like sliced down the middle and put in a hole.

Elyon raised her hand, wiggling her fingers in invitation. Larry didn't disappoint. Without pondering the inevitable consequences, he tried to wrap her in his huge arms. For a few seconds, Elyon allowed it to happen, wanting to be close enough to reach down and grab him by the balls.

For the space of a second, Larry grinned, unaware that he'd just lumbered into a trap.

Then Elyon squeezed her fingers and the man shrieked at a shrill octave that nearly burst Max's eardrums.

"So you tell me, bubba," Elyon said with a smug smile. "Do you think I'm tough?"

The man continued to scream as Max vaulted out of the ring and landed next to her.

"Elyon, don't play with them," he chided.

She sent him an overly innocent glance. "But it's so much fun."

"You're getting blood everywhere." He shook his head, his lips twitching. "And we haven't finished your tour."

"Fine."

She heaved a sigh, released her grip on the man's swollen 'nads and kicked him aside. Instantly Larry crumpled into a pile of quivering pain. Right next to his cousin who was still trying to stop the gush of blood from his nose.

Max shook his head, moving to lay a hand on Elyon's lower back.

"Come on, Rocky, the cages are this way," he said, steering her toward the heavy steel doors on the far end of the gym.

Wiping a splatter of blood off her chin, Elyon fell into step beside him. She wasn't even breathing hard, Max noticed. Damn. Kickass, and sexy as hell. A lethal combination. In all his time in captivity, he hadn't met a Pantera female. This one was truly something else, and he couldn't deny his overwhelming attraction to her.

"We need to get out of here," she whispered as he pushed open the doors and they stepped into the large, open space. Around the walls were rows of bleachers and in the center was a raised floor surrounded by ten-foot netting. At one time there had actually been steel cages, but as the sport became a million-dollar business, the sponsors of the matches had started to take care to ensure their best fighters weren't accidentally injured during a battle.

The smell of bleach hit him first, revealing that they'd already cleaned the area, although the lingering stench of old blood and sweat could still be detected. As if it'd been embedded in the very fabric of the room. He recoiled as he always did. The fucking smell...

"I can't leave," he told her, leading her to the edge of the cage.

She leaned forward, pretending to study the heavy mat. "Together we can get past any guards," she said. "Unless Victor has some secret security system?"

Max released a short laugh. "I'm not worried about the guards," he assured her. "And I'm sure the hell not worried about Victor. I could've left this shithole any time."

She sent him a puzzled glance. "Seriously? Then why do you want to stay?"

Want to stay? He almost laughed. Bitter and rage-filled. He was desperate to escape. But the price was far too high.

Although the gym wasn't nearly as bad as the torture he'd

suffered in Benson's lab, he hated every minute of it. The isolation. The brutal fights. The knowledge that the minute he left his loft apartment upstairs he was constantly on camera.

It wore his nerves raw.

But from the age of fifteen, he'd accepted that his life would no longer be his own.

"They have my parents," he said.

She straightened, eying him with an unreadable expression. "How long?"

"For years now. Too many goddamn years."

She exhaled heavily. "Where?"

He shrugged. "In New Orleans."

"Do you have the address?"

With a press of his hand, he urged her to move to the other side of the cage. At the same time, he studied her with a puzzled gaze.

Max frowned. He sensed that the questions weren't just casual conversation. She was searching for information.

"They move them around," he answered.

"Is there any way you can find out where they are right now?"

He halted, turning to face her. "What's going on?"

She bent down, studying the area beneath the cage in an effort to keep anyone watching them through the camera from reading her lips.

"If you can give me a location, I can have them rescued with one text."

Max laughed bitterly, then sobered as he took in her expression. "You're serious?"

She arched a brow. "Always."

"Why should I believe you?"

"Mmmm... You probably shouldn't."

It was all she said. No convincing, no assurance, no nothing. Crazy. He released a shaky breath. What the hell did he believe? For so many years he'd been responsible for the welfare of his parents. Every morning he woke up with the burden of knowing their security was dependent on his willingness to obey whatever order he was given by his captors.

It was staggering to imagine a future where they were free.

Or shit, himself.

But if it was possible…

With supreme effort, he squashed the urge to grab Elyon, look into her eyes, hard and desperate, then maybe kiss her in relief if he saw what he needed to see. Instead, he prayed he wasn't walking into a trap, and carefully considered the best way to share what little information he had.

His gaze skimmed the room, landing on the electronic equipment that was set up in the corner. Victor made additional money on the fights by streaming them to paying customers.

"Let's watch some TV," he said.

She sent him a startled glance. "What?"

He gave her a slow smile. "Come with me."

CHAPTER 5

Elyon absently followed behind Max, assuming that he had a plan. The majority of her brain was focused on his refusal to leave until he knew his parents were safe.

On one level she understood loyalty.

She would do anything for Raphael and the other members of The Six. But the fact that she'd been raised with no true family meant she struggled to fully comprehend the complexities of that dynamic. That bond.

Early on, guilt had been a constant knife in her gut. After all, if she had been a good female, a decent female, she would've gone looking for her mother and father as soon as she'd returned. Asked them questions, listened to their answers. Maybe forgiven them for not being the ones who'd found her. Or, if what she'd believed turned out to be true, for not searching for her every day that she'd been missing.

But things were different now. She rarely thought about them. She was...fine, good on her own. Great even. No burdens, no collateral damage if shit went south.

Max, however, had gone above and beyond. He'd remained imprisoned, been tortured and used, followed every order and demand, to keep his parents safe. He was clearly capable of true loyalty and deep love.

The thought made her feel a strange sort of longing.

"Here we go," Max said, pulling her from her thoughts.

He stood next to a long panel and was already flipping on switches. When he was done, he pulled out a phone from the pocket of his shorts and pressed his finger against the screen. A few swipes later he had a video pulled up and was syncing it to the gym's monitor, which was set at the end of the long table.

"I'll put on my last fight," he said in absent tones, still sliding his thumb over the screen of his phone. "That should keep the guards from wondering what we're doing."

Elyon wasn't sure what he was talking about, but before she could ask, the monitor flickered to life and the image of Max filled the screen. He was standing in the nearby cage, dressed like he was now, in a pair of loose shorts with his chest bare to reveal his stunning tattoos. A few feet away from him was a behemoth of a man. Six foot seven at least, with ropy muscles and a thick coating of hair over his body that made him look like a gorilla.

"Christ on a cracker," she breathed. "Where did they find your opponent?"

"Fresh meat from Siberia," Max said, not bothering to glance up. "He had an iron jaw, but one punch to the gut and he went down like a sack of potatoes." He crooked a finger at her. "Look at this."

Pressing close to his side, Elyon pretended to be watching the match on the monitor even as she covertly glanced toward his phone.

She could see an elderly couple with silver hair and the lined faces of people who'd lived through hardship. They were standing close together, their arms wrapped around each other as they stared at the camera with resigned expressions.

"Those are your parents?" she asked.

"Yes. Peter and Catherine Kudrow," he said, waving a hand toward the monitor as if they were discussing his fight. "I demand a picture to prove they're still alive at least once a week."

Elyon nodded. Smart of him to get proof of life. It made sure the enemy couldn't lie.

She turned her attention from the couple who had a faint resemblance to Max and instead studied what little she could see behind them.

"When did you get this one?" she asked.

"Just a couple hours ago."

She felt a flare of hope. "So there's a good chance they're still there?"

"That would be my guess," he agreed. "Usually they only move them once a month or so. They've been at this location less than a week."

"Good." She narrowed her gaze, staring at a blurry spot in the background. "Can you zoom in on the window behind your mother?"

"Yeah." Using his fingers, he enlarged the window to reveal the glowing sign of a restaurant that was next door.

"Abel's Po-Boys," she read out loud.

He glanced toward her, a wary hope in his eyes. "Do you know where it is?"

"Nope. But I can have someone find it." She pulled out her phone and typed out a swift message. Once she hit send, she put the phone back in her pocket and glanced at her companion with blatant impatience. "Now can we go?"

He stared at her, trying to read her. When she said no more, he put his phone away and folded his arms over his chest.

She sighed. "I'm thinking that's a no."

"Not until I'm sure they're safe," he said, his tone warning he wasn't going to argue. He wasn't budging until his parents were released.

Again she was fascinated by his fierce loyalty.

"You'd sacrifice your own freedom for them?" she asked in hesitant tones. "Even now?"

"Without hesitation."

She offered a slow nod.

He stared at her, curious. "Have you never loved, Elyon?"

The answer came, swift and unapologetic. "No."

"Not even your family?"

"I have none."

For a moment, his eyes remained on hers. They were deep amber and probing. "Well, I hope that changes. I hope you know love some day. It can chew you up and spit you out, for sure, but it's worth it in the end." His mouth softened. "My family is worth it. They're worth everything."

Elyon's heart swelled inside her chest at his words. She might not fully understand this love he spoke of, or his dedication to his parents, but she admired him with an intensity that was unnerving.

This was a male of worth.

Even if he hadn't been born Pantera.

He was—dare she even think it?—mate material.

Not that she was looking or wanting.

Job to do, Ely. "We have Hunters spread around New Orleans, but it could take an hour, maybe more, to rescue them," she warned, forcing a professional tone. With the current troubles plaguing her people, they'd pulled most of the Pantera back to the Wildlands. But there were always a few left in larger cities to keep track of what was happening among the humans. "It all depends on how well guarded they are."

He gave a jerky nod, his muscles rigid. Elyon sensed that he was battling to keep his emotions in check.

"It might be better if you leave and come back after my parents have been freed," he abruptly announced. "*If* they're freed."

What was he doing? Elyon scowled, glaring at him in disbelief. She'd traveled across the country to rescue him. Ensured that his parents would be taken away from their prison. And now he wanted her to leave?

First of all, she never left without an asset.

And secondly, she didn't want to. She was sort of enjoying being around him, looking at him, hearing him talk about his family.

And then there was that kiss…

She paused. Maybe that was it. Why he wanted her to leave.

After all, that kiss started as a way to shut her up. When the two idiots came in. Could it be that he didn't feel any of the instinctive urges to mate that were thundering through her?

Could he be completely turned off by her lack-of-love admission? Think she was cold?

Wouldn't he be right?

She lifted her chin. "Trying to get rid of me?"

His lips thinned, his expression hardening as he glanced at the old-fashioned dial clock on the wall.

"No, but Victor and his goons will be coming up here to prepare for tonight's matches," he said. "I don't like the thought of them bothering you." His jaw tightened and his eyes flashed as he turned back to face her. "You've been bothered enough for one day."

Her brows drifted up. *Oh.* He was…worried about her then? Well that was interesting. And better. Much better than what she'd cooked up in her head.

"You know I can take care of myself," she said with a hint of sass.

He moved in closer to her, his eyes darkening. "You've already proven that," he assured her. "But it doesn't change my desire…to protect you. Keep leering eyes off you."

An odd sensation clenched her heart. It didn't hurt exactly, but it made her a little breathless. She wished he'd take her hand or something. Maybe pull her in close, let her rub up against him, nuzzle his neck.

She licked her lips. His gaze was overpowering, magnetic, as he stared down at her. And his heat was searing her, drowning her in his male musk. Were these the leering eyes he was talking about? If so, she liked them. A lot. Wanted them on her. All night and day.

She lowered her voice. "You really want me to go, Max?"

He cocked his head, nostrils flaring as if trying to scent her. And when he did, when he pulled her into his lungs and exhaled, a soft, dangerous growl escaped his throat.

She smiled with satisfaction. "Do you live in the building?"

He nodded.

"Where?"

"Upstairs."

Her skin tingled with anticipation. "Are there cameras?"

He leaned in and whispered in her ear. "No."

She shivered.

"I told them I'd kill them if I discovered they were spying on my few hours of privacy." He eased back slowly, brushing his cheek against hers. "They were smart enough to know I wasn't bluffing."

"Well, I can wait there." Her lips twitched, and she bit the lower one.

His gaze dropped to her mouth. "Victor's going to wonder why you would want to go to my private rooms."

"Not if you come with me." A wicked smile curved her lips as she laid her palms flat against his chest and shoved him back against the wall. "Then he'll know exactly why I'm up there."

Max didn't touch her, but every inch of him was rigid with tension as he stared down at her, his musk permeating the air. Like he was holding on by a thread.

"Or," she whispered close to his mouth, "I can wait outside. Or maybe down in the restaurant. Have a bowl of borscht with those two idiots I bloodied. It'd be the right thing—"

His arms came around her so fast she gasped. But the sound quickly turned to sensual laughter as he lifted her up, tossed her over his massive shoulder, and started toward the stairs.

CHAPTER 6

Mine.

Mine, mine, mine.

It was like an anthem in his mind. The theme from "Rocky."

He felt like a fucking caveman taking her upstairs.

Or a Pantera male.

It was strange. Ever since she walked in, ever since his eyes touched down on her...everything, he was like a different man. Something volatile and hopeful. For years... No, *forever*, no one had come looking for him. No one had wanted to help him. No one had given two shits about him. And truly he'd gotten used it, and to the idea that the only road out of this nightmare was the one he traveled alone.

But...wow... Now she was here.

This creature of his dreams.

Rolling in like a beautiful, explosive storm, claiming she was a shifter, a liberator. Claiming she could fix his lifelong problems with one simple text. Claiming, with her eyes, her hands and her mouth that she wanted to consume him.

And to that, all Max could manage was one word.

Mine.

At the top of the stairs, he kicked open the door to his apartment with his foot. And once inside, kicked it shut.

"You going to put me down now, male?" she said, her voice teasing and warm.

He didn't answer. His body was too worked up. Already. And his mind...Well, shit was going on in there too. Questions, demands.

Stopping at the foot of the bed, he swung her off his shoulder and deposited her on the gray comforter. He was over her in seconds. His gaze pinned to hers.

"How do I know you're not full of shit?" he asked, hunger raging inside of him. "How do I know you're not a spy or a plant or a mole or just another way Benson's fucking with me?"

She stared up at him with those amazing dark blue eyes, breathing easy, utterly unafraid. "You don't."

Her confidence irritated him as much as it turned him on. "Why do the Pantera want me?"

"I don't know."

He shook his head. "That's a lie."

"I don't lie." She lifted her chin, trying to get closer to him, maybe get a taste, a kiss.

And fuck he wanted to give it to her.

"You're making this complicated," she pointed out. "It's very, very simple."

His dick was so hard now it felt like skin wrapped too tightly around liquid steel. It wanted her. Inside. Deep.

"My kind, whether you choose to believe it or not," she continued, "are good and honorable. That's what I know. *That* I believe with everything in my guts." She studied his face, her eyes probing him. "Max, I'm just trying to get you out of here, out of this life. Trying to get your parents free. It's not a trick, or veiled in anything—and I know that's hard to believe after what you've been through."

His jaw worked. Goddamn her for talking like this. So real. Believe it or don't. Take it or leave it.

He wanted to take it. Take her. Over and over.

She cocked her head just slightly. "But it's up to you. I think I've been pretty clear. About everything."

He didn't allow her one more word. His mouth was on her in seconds. Kissing her with all the heat and hunger and worry and anger and appreciation and hope that raged inside of him. That had lived inside of him for far too long. He gave it all to her. He gave it away. And she accepted it. With every lashing of his tongue, every bite to his lips, every deep, groan-filled kiss, she released it for him.

When he came up for air a minute or two later, he could hardly breathe. Hours in the ring with living monsters and hardened warriors and he barely broke a sweat, yet one drugging kiss from this female and he was fucking gasping.

"God, I want you," he whispered.

She grinned. Like a cat. "Then get your clothes off, and mine too, and let's do this."

Her words spoke to a part of him that had once been implanted, but was now threaded in his blood. "You know we could have company at any second."

Her grin widened. "I do."

A snarl of appreciation exited his lips. "Bad girl…" He sat up and started removing her boots, pitching each one aside.

"You have no idea, male," she uttered provocatively.

"I want to. I really, really want to." He drew down the zipper of her pants. "Female."

"Oh, I like that," she returned as he eased them off in one smooth stroke and tossed them over his shoulder.

A gruff curse broke from his lips as he saw she wore nothing underneath. Soft, smooth skin with just a thin strip of hair on her already glistening pussy.

"Like what you see?" she asked, dragging one leg to the side so he could get the full view.

"I don't care who it is," he said on a feral growl, his eyes lifting to meet hers. "I don't care if they're packing an Uzi or a firebomb. If someone walks in right now, sees you like this, I'll kill him."

Elyon sat up on her elbows. "The Pantera blood is strong in you."

Nostrils flared, eyes narrowed and fierce, he leaned forward and pulled the jacket from her shoulders, then eased the spandex top over her head. After tossing both away, he scooped her up and flipped her onto her stomach. She squealed and laughed hoarsely.

Max was beside himself now. The sight of her narrow waist and sweet, round ass nearly had him howling.

"Now you," she commanded. "Next time I see you, it better be all skin and hard muscle." And just to make him completely brain-dead, she raised that bitable backside and wiggled it at him.

Fuck... "Gone, done," he ground out as he ripped off the shorts and underwear he had on and pitched them at the window.

He leaned over her and settled his teeth on the hooks of her bra. For several long seconds, he just nuzzled her—her skin, the fabric, the little locks that stood between him and heaven on earth. She smelled like warmth and comfort and he wanted to just drown in her, and forget everything that came before her, and hell, maybe after her as well.

Jesus, this whole fucking thing was madness. How they'd met. Their instant connection. Her strength. His insane hunger.

Air rushed from his lungs as she lifted her ass again, and this time ground it hard against his shaft.

"Oh, Ely," he uttered, then ripped the fabric apart with his teeth. "What am I going to do with you?"

Even as he asked the question he was moving down her body, kissing and licking her hot skin as he went. She moaned and moved as he lightly bit between her shoulder blades, the center of her back, then kissing, down, down to her lower back.

The view. Christ. He planted himself just below her ass. She was a perfect, delectable angel. Sent from the Pantera, not heaven, but maybe that was better.

Sure was hotter.

He grazed his teeth over the round flesh, every inch of his body tight and tense. She made little mewling sounds, like the cat she was. And the strangest thing…each time she did, his chest vibrated. As if she was calling to something beneath his skin.

Impossible.

He moved downward, just a little, just enough so he could inhale her into his lungs. Beautiful. He gazed lovingly at her pussy. She was so wet, her lips glistening, her opening releasing sweet droplets of cream down her inner thighs.

Hunger assailed him.

Never had he felt like this.

Never had he wanted to taste and drink and feed from a female. But Elyon wasn't just a female. She was special. A work of art. A prize to be fought for and won.

With that thought, he dipped his head and lapped at the tears of her desire.

She hissed at the gesture and thrust her backside up, giving him an insane view. Tight, wet, and very pink folds. His heart stopped as he stared at the feast before him. It was like her pussy was calling to him.

Eat me.

Suck me.

Fuck me.

With gentle hands, he spread her ass cheeks and dipped his head, let his tongue run from her clit all the way to her sex. Her guttural groan was like the sweetest music, fueling him to give more, take more.

And he did.

Happily. Gratefully.

Again, he licked her from top to bottom, then back again, settling on the tight bud that was swelling even as he flicked it back and forth with the tip of his tongue. Eyes open, he watched as with each swipe, her pussy would clench and sweet juice would trickle out and tempt him.

"Mmmmmm," he whispered as he left her clit and licked all the way up to her opening. "You make me hungry, Elyon. But it's a hunger—no, a thirst—that will never be quenched.

This time, when he put his mouth on her hot, swollen bud and sucked her in, she cried out. He felt the sound everywhere. On his tongue, in his throat, under the skin of his chest, pulsing inside his cock. He kept at it, gently suckling her, drawing her clit inside, then releasing.

"Don't stop that, male," she commanded, her tone fierce, her breath labored. "Or I swear to the goddess I'll bite you."

He grinned and released her clit just enough to whisper, "That's no threat, Ely. That's an enticing promise."

She turned and glanced over her shoulder, snarled at him.

Max's eyes widened and his dick grew impossibly harder. She was a hot, sexy female, and yet...there it was, her puma, in her eyes, in the structure of her face.

Mine.

Max wasn't arguing with whatever that was inside of him. Not anymore. It'd be a lie.

His tongue came out and as he stared at her, he flicked her clit back and forth. Her nostrils flared and against his tongue he felt her tremble. Again, he lapped at her. Back and forth. Over and over until the trembling extended to her legs and her ass and her back.

She let her head fall forward and lifted her backside even higher.

Max gripped her ass in his palms and nestled his face in her pussy, drinking, sucking, moving with her as she pumped her hips wildly. She was going to come. He was going to make this incredible female fly over the edge of blissful madness.

No. We are.

No longer was it a voice in his head, but a snarl inside his chest. And ignoring it was impossible. *They* were hungry. *They* wanted to feed from her.

Holding on tight, he sucked her until her manic jerks ceased, until she froze and cursed and creamed and cried out into the room he'd never brought anyone to—his quiet prison.

Max knew bliss.

Her wet heat permeated his nostrils, marked him, and with each gentle flick to her clit he took her from the top of the mountain peak down to the soft, warmth of the valley.

She shivered and shook, and he released her and gave her ass a soft kiss.

He was just about to pull her into his arms, when she suddenly flipped onto her back, wrapped her arms around his torso and rolled them both over.

Max grunted with the movement, then groaned as he took in the sight before him.

Or above him.

Elyon sat on his thighs, her legs spread wide as she straddled him. She looked like a fierce, sexy predator, hungry for her prey. From her beautiful face to her sleek shoulders, to her breasts, her flat stomach, and the nearly shaved pussy that was wet and ready for him, he'd never desired anything more.

She was a goddess.

"Ely," he murmured, needy as fuck.

She smiled and took his cock in her hand. "Your turn."

***

As she sat poised above Max, Elyon still shook from her climax. Still breathed heavily. She'd never been touched that way before. So raw, untamed, so hungry. Like it would never be enough, yet would always be enough. There was no question in her mind now. This male was her match. She was convinced of it. How it happened she didn't know. How he'd softened her heart so swiftly, when that muscle had been surrounded by iron walls for…forever, she wasn't sure. But now, as she looked down on this fearsome male, with his black braid, his angel wing tattoo, his amber eyes rimmed by midnight black lashes, full mouth, and hard jaw, she felt a strange, feminine weakness.

Until he started stroking his cock, that is.

Control. Back.

She grinned. He was beautiful. In every way. Long, hard as metal, and leaking at the top—she felt her mouth water...or was that her sex? Her fingers tightened on him, trying to fully encircle him. But it was no use. He was too thick.

"Want," she snarled.

"This?" he asked, placing his hand over hers.

Her eyes clung to the thick, pink organ that stood straight up, and their stacked hands. This time, he set the pace. Guiding her hand up and down, squeezing as they drew closer to the base.

His groan rent the air and in seconds, his hands were on her hips. He lifted her into the air and held. Breathless and smiling with delight, she stared down. Muscles, sweat, tight, hard. His strength was formidable, hot as hell. Precious few could match her, much less overpower her in bed like he no doubt could.

She looked forward to that day. Pinned down, maybe her wrists tied...

It was her turn to groan, and just as she did, he started to lower her. But it was slow...too slow. Her sex clenched in anticipation, and she growled at him.

He chuckled, the sound vibrating through her. "Patience, my beautiful cat."

"Oh," she whispered as the head of him entered her. "Oh, goddess, yes."

It was like Christmas morning. A new present each glorious inch he gave her. And there were many presents in store. He was huge. And she deserved no less.

Mine.

Yeah, yeah, she told her cat. *Wait your turn.*

All thoughts died in her mind then as he not only set her down on his shaft, but grabbed her shoulders and pressed himself deeper still.

For long seconds, she couldn't breathe.

It was fucking glorious.

Max's eyes were near to black. No longer amber. *His cat's eyes.* He released her shoulders and dragged his hands down her to her breasts. His lip lifting with his soft snarl, he palmed them both and started to massage them.

Ely arched her back and pushed herself closer to him. "We fit," she uttered breathlessly.

"Like a glove," he agreed, his fingers working her nipples.

A rush of heat thrashed her insides and she started to move, rotating her hips, slow circles to feel him everywhere.

"I can't believe this is happening," she said on a whimper.

"I can."

Her eyes refocused on him.

He grinned wickedly up at her. "From the first moment I saw you, I knew you were the kind of female who took what she wanted."

"You think I wanted you, male?" She reached for him, one hand on his chest, which felt like skin over steel, and the other grabbing at his braid.

His eyes went wide and he growled at her, sending his hips up and thrusting his cock so deeply inside of her she gasped.

"Didn't you?" he taunted. "Christ knows I wanted you. Desperately. Like air to a dying man."

Ely could barely hear him now. With that thrust, he'd sent her into another world. She was herself there, yes, but she was her cat too, and everything was brighter and hotter and wetter.

Closing her eyes, she started to move, starting riding him. The build up inside of her was overwhelming and uncomfortably wonderful now, and she wanted the finish line she craved.

"Oh, fuck, Ely," he groaned, grabbing her hips and matching her movement. "I wish you could see what I see. Straddling me like that, your sexy, wet pussy taking my cock deep, belly contracting with the need to come. Oh, Christ, yes, woman… Nipples hard, pulse pounding in your throat. And your face," he groaned as she moved faster, pulled his braid harder. "So beautiful.

You're no angel of death. You're my angel of life."

And with those words, that wonderful, personal sentiment, Elyon hit the pinnacle. Crying out, she gave herself over to wave upon wave of delicious, almost painful ecstasy. She felt Max's hands on her hips, guiding her thrusts as he neared the edge, and was so grateful. Her strength was waning, her mind was fuzzy, every inch of her skin was trembling with electric fire…

"Elyon," Max snarled. "Look at me."

Her mouth parted and she shook her head, groaning.

"Look at me now!" he demanded.

Her eyes shot open, just in time to watch him climax. As she was coming down, he was flying high. His face was hard and ferocious, and as he pounded into her, taking, claiming, she saw something. Just below the surface of his skin…in his eyes.

His cat.

Beautiful.

Majestic.

Mine, growled the mated and very possessive cat inside her.

CHAPTER 7

As he held the female—his female—in his arms, Max knew that life would never be the same.

It was that simple.

And that profound.

But even as he struggled to accept just how deeply he'd been altered since Elyon had strolled into the gym with her badass attitude and sexy grin, he realized that he knew precious little about her.

The thought bothered him.

Not because they didn't have the rest of their lives to become better acquainted. Oh, he'd be making sure of that. Eventually he would discover her favorite color and if she liked coffee black or with sugar and cream. But he sensed that the barriers she used to keep others at a distance hadn't been completely lowered, despite the raw intimacy of their sex.

There were pieces she continued to keep hidden from him.

Brushing his lips over her sweaty brow, he wrapped his arms even tighter around her naked body. "Tell me, Ely."

He could practically feel her smile. "What?"

"About you."

She turned her head so she could plant openmouthed kisses over his chest.

"Boring," she said in husky tones. "I can think of better ways to spend our time."

His body hardened, in instant agreement with her unspoken suggestion of how they could be spending their time.

But that would come. Later.

With a low growl he rolled to pin her beneath his large body, grabbing her wrists to pull her arms above her head.

"You might be able to deflect everyone else, but not me," he warned, leaning down until they were nose to nose. "I'm stubborn enough to break through your walls."

"I bet you are," she whispered, canting her hips. "I think you should break through my walls right now."

"Ely," he warned.

She bared her teeth, hissing at him. "You're being tiresome. There's nothing to say."

He swallowed the urge to laugh. She was such a cat. Instead, he growled right back at her.

Clearly, they were going to have a constant skirmish to see who was alpha. It was a battle he looked forward to with savage anticipation.

"You say you have no family," he started. "What happened to your parents?"

Wariness darkened her eyes.

He tightened his grip on her wrists. "Come on, female. Give me something here."

"They're not in the picture," she ground out.

He released an exasperated sigh. "That answer sucks."

"Well, it's the only one I have."

"I doubt that."

There was a long silence and he took the opportunity to move down a few inches and take one of her nipples into his mouth. After a sharp suckle, he whispered against the pointy tip, "You're going to talk to me. This can't work, we can't work, unless you open up and let me see who you really—"

"Fine. My parents are dead, and I was kidnapped when I was five, okay?" The words came out in a breathy rush.

Max stilled. *Well…shit.* That wasn't what he'd been expecting. He left her breast and lifted his eyes to meet hers again. Her suddenly pale face bothered him, and he stared at her with open sympathy. Granted, he hadn't been kidnapped, but he understood the pain of being violently separated from his family. It'd left wounds that he wasn't sure would ever fully heal.

"I'm sorry, about your parents," he said. "Was it Benson Enterprises? Who took you?"

She gave a slow shake of her head. "No, it was a few local assholes who were hoping to blackmail my parents for my return."

Her voice was completely stripped of emotion, he noticed. Which warned him that this was definitely a traumatic moment in her life. It was a pattern with her. The more she emotionally vulnerable she felt, the more aggressively she tried to pretend it meant nothing.

"It wasn't until after they'd snatched me that they realized I wasn't...normal."

Although he'd been made a Pantera by blood infusions, Max had seen a few of the pure Pantera male children who had been brought to the lab. They'd been vicious fighters who'd been able to take out more than one guard. He'd always wondered what had happened to them. Maybe he'd find out.

"Did you bite them?" he asked.

Fierce satisfaction settled on her face. "Maybe once or twice."

"Good." He studied the shadows that lurked in the back of her eyes. Her memories haunted her, perhaps even more than his did. Maybe because she hadn't dealt with them. "What happened after you were taken?"

She licked her lips and released an irritated breath, clearly wanting to tell him to go to hell. Deep-seated distrust flickered in her eyes. She didn't open up, to anyone, he'd be willing to bet.

"They took me to the jungle and dumped me in the river. Are we done now?"

Max sucked in a sharp breath and released her arms. He took her face in his hands. It was impossible to imagine being just five years old and not only being ripped from your family but tossed in the middle of a jungle.

It didn't matter if she was Pantera or not.

"Damn." Sympathy twisted his gut into a tight knot. "You were just a baby."

She shrugged. "It was fine. I may not have been able to release my cat, but she helped me to survive anyway—until I was taken in by a local village."

He wasn't fooled for a second by her nonchalant tone. How did he get in there? Her heart? "You must have been terrified."

Her lashes swept downward, hiding her eyes. "Like I said, I survived."

Anger blasted through him. Frustration too. She wouldn't be broken. Those walls. Those damned walls she kept not only building, but fortifying. Hell, he'd shared his nightmare with her. If this was going to happen between them, she needed to be able to trust him, open up to him.

"Why can't you just admit that you were frightened to be a child alone in the wilderness?" he pressed. He waited for her to meet his glare. When she didn't, he leaned down to nip her lower lip in warning. "Elyon?"

She muttered a curse, then her lashes lifted to reveal eyes that glowed with annoyance.

"Yes, I was afraid," she snapped. "Satisfied?"

Max ignored her burst of temper. He suspected that trying to earn her trust was going to be an ongoing battle. But he'd win. He was a stubborn beast.

"No," he said bluntly. "I don't like when you do that."

She blinked, almost as if she didn't even realize that she'd so effectively shut him out.

"Do what?"

He held her gaze, his fingers tightening around her wrists. "You're not allowed to hide your emotions from me."

She pressed her lips together, eying him with blatant suspicion. "Most males are happy not to have to deal with emotions."

He bent his head, pressing his lips against hers in a fierce kiss. "I'm not most males."

She melted against him. "True."

He continued to kiss her. No battles of the tongue and teeth. Just slow, drugging passion to share as their flesh heated up once again.

"No more hiding," he commanded, lifting his head to study her flushed face with a brooding gaze. "Deal?"

She wrinkled her nose. "I'll try."

His lips twitched with humor. *What a shocker. She's stubborn too.* "Who finally came for you? Who found you? A Pantera?"

She was caught off guard by the question. "Yes, Raphael found me."

Without warning, Max was the one who was fighting back a surge of anger. A male's name had crossed her lips. After he'd just tasted them. He didn't like the way her features had softened and her scent deepened at the mention of— "Raphael?" he ground out.

One eyebrow drew up at his fierce tone. "He's the leader of our species. Of the Pantera."

"Is he your lover?" he snarled.

"No, of course not," she breathed in shock. "He has a mate and a small daughter."

"But you care about him," he pressed.

"He's a friend. A mentor." She lifted her head to brush her lips along the line of his tense jaw. "A member of the *sort of* family I mentioned before."

His eyes were pinned to hers, and he felt like his guts were twisting. And that thing under his chest, that vibrating thing was sending up shots of adrenaline and possessiveness.

"Hey, dude," she said, smiling up at him wickedly. "Where's that trust you want from me?"

On a soft growl, Max released her wrists, and spread her legs with his thigh. "Maybe we'd better talk about what we are, Ely."

Her eyes instantly softened and sparkled. "Oh, yes. Let's do that. Let's *talk*."

"I'm serious."

"I know you are."

He rose up and entered slowly, stretching her with each inch, before halting and holding himself there. "Who you belong to. Who I belong to."

The warm heat of her, the way her muscles closed around him and squeezed, his mind threatened to explode. But he forced the thing to remain clear. He wanted an answer from her, needed it.

She reached for him, for his braid, which had fallen over one shoulder. Slowly, almost lovingly, she pulled off the band and released his hair. The long black strands fell forward and made a curtain around them.

"Wow," she breathed, wrapping her legs around his waist and holding on tight. "You are something else, Max." Her eyes lifted to meet his. "And make no mistake, you belong to me. Have from the second I walked into this place."

He growled at her.

"Now, show me," she said with a smile. "Prove it. Mark me. Not on the outside of my body like some in our world. But inside." Her eyes flashed with the heat of her cat. "Deep."

Mind.

Blown.

Gone.

Hers.

And as the night outside grew darker still, he thrust into the female he was certain would rule his heart for eternity. Just as she'd commanded: deep, marking her well and good as he buried himself in every inch of her hot, creamy walls.

CHAPTER 8

Elyon pulled her shirt over her head, then grabbed her boots. She'd taken a quick shower to wake her sex-addled brain, though she'd wanted to keep his scent on her for as long as possible. Maybe when they returned to the Wildlands, she'd shove him up against a wall again. Or hell, on the plane ride home. Those bathrooms were just the right size for one standing, one on their knees.

She was desperate to taste him.

That long, thick—

Her phone vibrated on the low nightstand, cutting off her oh-so heavenly thoughts. After shoving her foot in her remaining boot, she reached for it.

Thanks, E. 2 fists to my very pretty face & a bullet that grazed my ass.

She rolled her eyes at Leo's dramatics. **Did you get them?**

Who or what do you think I am?

Dangerous question, bro. Lab's still not back w/the results.

Ha ha. Fuck u.

She laughed, feeling a strange, new sensation. Happiness? Satisfaction? Possibility? Whatever it was, she could figure it out later. Right now, they were so out of here, and *yippee!* she would get her sweaty plane time sooner than expected.

Nice people, btw. Scared shitless.

Not surprised. Been through hell.

Ok. On our way to the meeting point. C U.

"What's going on?" Max moved to stand behind her, his massive arms loosely wrapping around her waist as he nuzzled her neck.

Elyon went soft and warm in seconds. She pressed back against his chest, marveling at how easy it was to accept his strength, his possession. Only hours ago she would have kicked the ass of anyone stupid enough to try and hold her so intimately.

"Your parents are safe."

She felt a tremor race through his body and turned to face him. He was a fearsome thing. A true warrior. Dark, dangerous, broad, and bad, his black hair loose around his shoulders. She knew just how he would be in the ring. Merciless. Tireless. But right then, gazing down at her he looked...young. Vulnerable.

"You're sure?" he asked, his voice threaded with disbelief.

"See for yourself." She held up her phone, pressing on the video that had just hit her inbox. *Thank you, Leo, even though you're a douchebag most of the time.*

Instantly the image of an older couple became visible. It looked like they were seated in the back of a moving car, their lined faces wreathed with smiles even as their eyes remained dark with concern.

"Max, we're on our way to something called the Wildlands," his mother said, leaning toward the camera as if physically willing her son to listen to her plea. "Please get out of that awful place. We're safe, and we love you."

A rough sound wrenched from Max's throat, and he did the strangest, most amazing thing. He let his head drop to her shoulder.

The gesture did something to her. Unraveled her. Like she'd been a ball of twine—always been a ball of twine—since she was just five and was stolen away from all that she knew.

Tightly bound.

But this male was slowly tickling the frayed edges of that twine, encouraging her, making her believe she was both needed and wanted. Making her crave a connection that was far deeper than friendship or even what she had always believed mating to be.

With Cerviel, with all of the Pantera, she'd thought taking a mate was a normal progression of time, and the body's understanding that it had found its sexual equal.

Well, it was true she'd definitely found that. In fact, she was going to have to eat a lot of protein to keep up with this one. But as Max lifted his head and found her gaze, she knew why Cerviel had acted the way he had outside the safe house, why he didn't seem to give a shit if Raphael kicked him out of The Six. Why he wouldn't leave Hallie for anything. Real and true mating fused hearts for life.

Even damaged ones.

Perhaps most especially damaged ones.

She ran comforting hands up and down the curve of his broad back. He'd showered too and he smelled good, soap and his unique Pantera musk. In turn, he leaned in and pressed a soft kiss to the side of her neck.

"You ready, baby?" he said against her skin.

She shivered. No one called her those names, those endearments. She hadn't allowed it. But with him, all she said was, "Always." *For you. Always.*

Raking his teeth over the thin band of muscle at her neck, he groaned. "You're going to be my addiction. Wanting more. Never enough."

"Let's hope so."

He eased back and gave her a hungry grin. "My Ely."

Yes.

Then he planted a quick kiss on her mouth before he released her.

She watched as he pulled on a pair of gray sweats over his boxers, and a matching hoodie over the most beautiful chest ever created.

"Why did you get the angel wings?" she asked him.

He paused. "Pretty simple actually. I wanted to cover the scars of my imprisonment with a symbol of my freedom."

Not twenty-four hours ago, Elyon would've nodded at that answer. Made sense. Moving on. That sort of thing. But tonight, her eyes fixed on her mate, her heart his for the taking and the holding, she felt a pull...from her insides to his. Her cat to his. Her soul to his. She knew what true freedom felt like after not having it for so long. And she was so thankful he had it now.

Max slid his feet into a pair of sneakers and looked at her expectantly. "We're out of here."

She glanced around the loft. "You don't want to pack a bag?"

He sent her an intimate smile. "The only thing in this room that means anything to me is you."

There it was. Again. That connection, running through her at hyper-speed. A beautiful ache that she never wanted to have healed. It was the heart inside her chest that she'd honestly believed dead—but now knew was only dormant—blooming.

She knew the true reason she'd traveled to New York. To deliver the asset. But things had changed. Drastically. She wanted to protect him as much as bring him home. One question hovered on her tongue.

"Has Victor ever mentioned why you're special, Max?"

He flicked a brow upward. "I thought I just proved why I'm special."

Heat fizzed through her like champagne that had been shaken.

Damn him. But, boy was he was right. He had been special.

Epically special.

Focus, Ely. With great effort, she continued. "Have they ever mentioned using your blood in any experiments? Or suggested training you for a secret project?"

He shrugged, his gaze curious now. "No. Where are you going with this?"

"Not sure. Just think. Please."

He sighed. "They just want me to fight and bring in lots of money, baby." He hesitated then, as if struck by a sudden thought. "Victor did mention something about sending me to Vegas to fight within the next couple of days. I assumed it was for a televised match."

Oh, Victor, you're so tricky. More likely it was a ruse so Max wouldn't be suspicious when they loaded his hot ass into a van so they could take him some place quiet to kill him and dispose of his body. A task that wouldn't be so easy in the middle of the city.

The mere thought of Max being murdered, being taken from her, was enough to splinter her blood-deep sense of duty to the PSL. She was never leaving his side, no matter what Raphael said.

"Let's go," she said. Any further questions could wait until she had this male hidden in a safe house. Far away from Benson and his nefarious plans. Under her eagle-eyed watch.

With a small nod toward Max, she waited for him to head toward the door. She followed as he walked out of the loft and headed down the narrow flight of stairs.

Her muscles tensed, her cat pressing beneath her skin. Who knew what they were going to encounter? She could already hear the sounds of voices in the gym, no doubt competitors preparing for the nightly cage matches. Which she was supposed to have been headlining.

Whoops.

They reached the main floor no problem, but even as they prepared to try and slip unnoticed through the back area where the cage was set up, Max reached out to grasp her arm.

"In here," he commanded under his breath, tugging her into a small storage closet beneath the stairs.

Ugh. This was no airplane bathroom. They were crammed into a tiny space that reeked of old mats and moldering boxing gloves. Thankfully Max kept the door open a few inches to allow in some fresh air, as well as giving them a glimpse of the two large men who jogged across the floor and headed directly up the stairs.

"What's going on?" Elyon whispered.

Max shook his head, his eyes narrowed as he watched the half dozen men who spilled through the door across the gym.

"I don't know, but something's up," he said, his tone threaded with unease. "There's never this many guards on duty at the same time."

Elyon grimaced. It didn't take a genius to figure out why there would be a sudden overflow of beefy security in the gym. Raphael was going to string her up for not getting Max out of there right away, against his will or not. She was so not looking forward to that conversation, and the questions about what exactly she was doing during that time.

"They must know your parents have escaped," she whispered.

Max nodded, his expression grim. Before he could speak however, the heavy sound of footsteps pounding back down the stairs echoed through the storage room. Then Victor's voice floated through the air.

"Did you find him?" the older man demanded.

"He's not there," a harsh voice responded.

Was that the same idiot Elyon had met downstairs? Probably, although she couldn't see more than his shoes and one leg through the small crack.

She inhaled deeply, seeing if she could capture his scent over the mold and rank. Not possible. Though gagging was.

"What the hell do you mean?" Victor snapped.

"I mean he's not there," the man insisted.

There was a long string of curses before Victor managed to regain his composure. "What about the woman?"

"Gone," the guard admitted.

Another spat of swearing as Victor paced back and forth, allowing Elyon fleeting glimpses of his florid face. He was clearly pissed off.

"Benson is going to slit my throat when he finds out I let Max escape. He might have let me have an extra week to make some money on the bastard, but when he realizes I didn't complete the elimination process exactly as he demanded..." his words trailed off with a violent shiver before he was giving a loud clap of his hands. On cue the muscle-bound guards hurried to stand in front of him. Like a pack of well-trained dogs. *Pant, pant, pant.* "They can't have gone far," Victor said in a loud voice. "Check the security tapes and then spread out and look for them."

So maybe Victor was an enemy of the Pantera after all.

Elyon could already taste his ancient blood.

One of the nearest guards had pulled out a handgun. "Lethal force?" he demanded, a hint of anticipation in his voice.

Max grunted. Clearly the two men weren't BFFs.

"You can kill the woman," Victor said. "I need Max alive. At least until we can take him to the meeting place."

Well! How rude. But even as she thought the quip, Elyon tucked away the information. The message Xavier had intercepted back in the Wildlands had ordered the test subjects to be destroyed, but it seemed that Victor had received another message with specific details on exactly how Max was to be killed.

So why was Max different?

Was it because a dead body in the building owned by Benson might cause unwanted questions? That made sense. It wasn't like anyone here had the brains to come up with a suitable reason there was a dead man in their gym.

Or maybe they just worried about the fights being shut down by the authorities.

Whatever the reason, she had to get them out of there.

Now.

Elyon watched as the men exchanged glances, clearly not

super excited about the thought of trying to capture Max "The Hammer" without being able to put a bullet through his brains.

Maybe they weren't as stupid as they looked.

"But—" One of them started to protest only to snap his lips shut as Victor pointed a stubby finger in his direction.

"Did I ask for your opinion?"

"No, sir."

"Then go. And don't come back to me without him."

***

Max waited until the guards had scurried away, and Victor had stormed back to his office before he eased open the door to the storage room.

Most of the security guys would head downstairs, assuming that they'd already left the gym and were trying to get out of the building.

Which meant that the only way would be to go up.

He bent his head, speaking directly in Elyon's ear. "We'll go out the fire escape."

She nodded, stepping back and waving for him to go out of the closet first. He smiled, knowing just how much trust it took for her to allow him to take the lead. But she was also smart enough to know he knew every inch of this place.

In silence, they hugged the shadows of the back edge of the gym. It was eerily silent. Usually by this hour the fighters were crowding into the locker room while a steady stream of paying customers were filing up the stairs. Obviously Victor had shut the place down for the night.

They managed to reach the doors leading to the cage room, and were headed toward a heavily barred window at the far end when their luck ran out.

There was the squeak of the old floorboards before a bald-headed guard stepped out of a side door. The man looked momentarily startled, as if he was shocked that he'd actually managed to locate Max and Elyon. Had he chosen to remain up here because he didn't want to risk a fight? Maybe. But the moment he caught sight of them, his sense of duty overcame any reluctance and he pointed a finger in their direction.

"Hey. Stop right there," he commanded.

Max glanced toward Elyon who was already spreading her legs as she prepared to fight.

"I'll take care of him," he told her. "You need to get that window open without tripping the alarms."

She hesitated, glancing toward the guard before giving a sharp nod of her head. She obviously determined that he could handle one human guard.

Pivoting, she swiftly moved toward the window. The guard muttered an oath, reaching to his side to awkwardly pull his handgun.

Max rolled his eyes. The dumbass was going to shoot himself by accident. Not that Max minded. One less idiot in the world. But the shot would attract unwanted notice.

With one long leap, he was standing directly in front of the guard, knocking the weapon from his hands before the man even realized he'd moved. With a yelp of shock, the man stumbled back, putting up his hands.

Max studied the guard's movements, not about to underestimate him as a threat. The only fight he'd ever lost was to a man who was six inches shorter and a hundred pounds lighter. The fighter had pretended to be terrified in the cage and Max had stupidly led with his chin, barely seeing the punch coming before he was knocked flat on his ass.

Now he gave a quick right jab, watching as the man ducked to the left, his weight on his heels instead of the balls of his feet.

Max gave another right jab quickly followed by a kick toward the man's knee. The guard skipped backward, avoiding the kick and throwing a left hook at Max.

Max easily ducked, using the motion to move in closer. The man wasn't much taller than Max, but he had an inch or two longer arm. A decided advantage in a boxing match.

The guard realized his mistake a beat too late. His head jerked back even as Max's massive fist smashed into his jaw. The man choked out a cry of pain, but he didn't go down as Max had expected. Instead he lowered his head and abruptly lunged forward.

Max was forced to dance backward, nearly stumbling over a folding chair that had been left near the cage. It was only a momentary distraction, but it gave the guard the advantage.

The man smiled, wrapping his arms around Max's neck and squeezing with his considerable power. On a normal man the press of the guard's forearm might have crushed his throat. Or at least cut off his air supply.

But Max wasn't normal. He returned the man's smile just before he jerked his head forward, slamming the crown of his skull directly to the center of the guard's face.

There were all kinds of snaps and pops as bones broke and cartilage was shattered. The guard gave a pig-like squeal before he was stumbling backward and covering his busted face with his hands.

Max was still smiling when he picked the man up and bench-pressed his two-hundred-pound body over his head. Then, with one mighty heave, he was tossing the guard through the air to smash against the wall.

There was a satisfying crack as the man's head connected with the wall of cement, then he was sliding down to land on the floor with a heavy thud.

There was the sound of a clicking tongue and Max turned his head to discover Elyon regarding him with raised brows.

"Showing off?"

His lips twitched as he moved to kick the man onto his back, ensuring he was unconscious.

Yep. Out cold.

"Maybe a little," he agreed, jogging across the room to join her at the window that was already opened. "Turn you on?"

Her eyes flashed with heat. "You have no idea."

He pressed a kiss to her lips. "Let's get the fuck out of here, baby."

"Agreed," she murmured, turning to climb onto the rickety fire escape.

Within seconds they were on top of the building, heading for the edge. The wind was fierce, but the lights of the city sparkled like gems. Like beacons of promise.

As soon as she had Max stashed in the hotel room she'd booked earlier, she would return and exterminate the pests.

Quietly and efficiently.

They weren't smart enough to flee. Like rats returning to their nest.

Truly, that would be far less messy than blowing up the entire place, even though she really did love to pull that plug when vermin were involved. But it would offer her the opportunity to search through their computers for any information that would tell them why Benson was so eager to get rid of the test subjects.

The plan had barely formed in her mind when there was a sound of a heavy 'thud' quickly followed by the shake of the building beneath their feet.

Holy shit, no. Come on! Someone had found her explosives. Or maybe they'd brought some of their own.

Whichever it was, the entire place was about to blow.

"Jump," she rasped.

Max didn't need her urging. He was already swiftly behind her, leaping to the neighboring building. And then the next.

Bet you're loving that Pantera blood now, baby!

Behind them, the ear-piercing sound of a massive explosion sent shockwaves through the air. Neither turned to look as the Benson building was destroyed in a blast of shattered brick, melted iron, and jagged glass.

Instead they dodged the projectiles that flew over two blocks, as they disappeared into the darkness.

Someone was clearly willing to flatten the building rather than allowing the secrets hidden inside to be revealed, Elyon mused as she followed Max down a new and far less rickety fire escape. Now the question was…who was responsible, and what secrets were worth such destruction?

Ely shook her head, reaching behind her to grab Max's hand as they entered the building through an open office window. He offered it instantly. Team players. Mates.

For now, nothing mattered but the fact that they'd managed to escape.

Tomorrow was time enough to worry about the future.

CHAPTER 9

"You're shitting me, right? You've mated? Your asset?"

As dawn broke all around her, Elyon tried to ignore Cerviel. She was hot and dusty, her new boots had a hole in the toe from that last roof to roof leap, and she desperately wanted a swim in the cool bayou. But her dark-eyed, goatee-loving ghost brother wasn't having any of it. He'd brought his A game to the party, and wasn't going home without retribution.

The A game being Advanced mockery.

And the party being the safehouse just outside the Wildlands.

No hotel room for her and her male. Sad.

Course, she probably deserved Cerviel's censure. Not too long ago, she'd ripped him a new one for falling head over ass for the female he'd rescued in Wyoming. She'd thought he was a fool. No, she'd thought he was a traitor.

Her lashes lifted and she caught sight of her man, her male, sitting by the water's edge. For the past thirty minutes, he hadn't moved. Just sat there, bracketed by his mother and father, one thickly muscled arm around each of their shoulders.

Her gut twisted. He hadn't seen them in years. And yet they'd been all he could think about, care about. Enduring terrible pain and imprisonment just to keep them safe.

And what had she done?

Taken too long to decide.

She released a weight breath. And believed they hadn't loved her enough to find her. She'd been so damn stubborn, so jaded, she hadn't even gone to them and found out.

Something hot and wet stung her eyes, but she swiped it away

168

quickly. Before Cerviel could see.

That's what was wrong with her. That's why she never felt or cared or trusted until Max came along. She was punishing herself. She didn't deserve peace or joy because she'd never given her parents the chance to explain—anything! She'd never given them the chance to hold her close and apologize for giving up and believing she was never coming back.

They went to their graves not even knowing she was alive.

"Hey," Cerviel pressed near her ear. "I want to hear about this grand romance and of course, the building you blew up."

"I didn't blow it up." She did wonder who had, though.

"Spill."

"Oh my goddess! I have nothing to say to you, okay?" She turned away from the beautiful familial scene, from Cerviel, from her guilt and shame and all the other feelings she'd never allowed herself, and headed around the back of the house. She wanted a second alone. To stare into the wetlands and just breathe in the moist air.

But Cerviel was on the warpath.

"Shouldn't you be with your mate?" she ground out, whirling around to face him. "And not bothering people."

He was completely unfazed by her vitriol. "She's sleeping, and you know how much I enjoy bothering you. Especially when you so royally fucked up."

In more ways than you can know. She glared at him. "You did the same thing."

"And you reamed me out for it."

"It's a bonehead move. On both our parts." She crossed her arms over her chest and tried to muster up some frostiness. "We should be kicked out of the PSL. Raphael would have every right."

"Of course he would," Cerviel agreed, his black eyes annoyingly clever. "Then you'd leave for parts unknown and lover boy over there would stay here."

"I'm going to shave that goatee off of your smug face with my claws," she threatened, shaking her head.

"You'll have to shift first. And to do that, you need to get closer to the Wildlands. And if what you predict comes true, you'll be going bye bye." His lips curved into an arrogant grin. "Maybe you should say your goodbyes now. Before he's called in for his examination. Which, by the way, is being done by Monique today. Remember her? Petite redhead with the gigantic—"

She had him against the back door of the safehouse in seconds.

He laughed. "It was the Monique thing, right? Sent you over the edge."

"I hate you," she ground out.

"No, you don't. You hate that I'm telling the truth. If that male is yours, claim him. To Raphael, to everyone. And let the chips fall where they may."

She groaned and released him. "Ram is going to kill us."

He snorted. "Probably. But what's the alternative? Be without them? No fucking way." He studied her for a moment, then shook his head. "You love this guy."

Yes. "He's not a guy. He's a male. And my feelings are my own."

"Sure they are."

There was a long silence, where they both just stared out at the cypress as the breeze blew around them.

"Cerviel?" she said.

"Yeah?"

"I don't even know what it is, or what it means."

"Love?"

"I've never felt it. For anyone."

He sniffed and turned to face her. "Does the idea of being without him, even for a day, make your insides bleed?"

"Try an hour."

He smiled gently. "Then you know what it is, Ely."

"What does Elyon know?" came a male voice she and her cat

knew soul-deep.

Elyon turned to see that male she couldn't be away from standing there, all six feet six inches of him. Her gorgeous male warrior. He looked tired, and a bit beat up from their roof jumps, but a good kind of tired. Like maybe he could finally release a breath after so many years of holding it tight inside his lungs.

"Wow," Cerviel observed. "He's a big one."

She grinned.

Mine.

"I am," Max said, then added, "And don't you forget it." Though the warning lacked heat.

Coming to his feet, Cerviel replied good-naturedly, "I'm no threat, buddy. Ely's like a sister. So, you know, gross."

She rolled her eyes and flipped him the bird.

He laughed as he started away. "I'm going to go check on my sleeping beauty. Wake her up with a kiss. Etcetera."

"Okay," Elyon called after him, "now it's my turn to say gross."

When she glanced back, Max was in front of her, offering her his hand. "Want to go for a walk? Show me this place? Or the outskirts, at any rate."

Happily, eagerly, she took it, and let him help her to her feet. "What about your parents?"

"Raphael found them a cottage down the way. They're exhausted. Going to let them rest for a bit."

"Sounds like a good idea for all of you. I'm sure you're tired too."

His eyes were warm; so was his hand. "Come, Ely."

She smiled at him and chided, "Is this your first demand of me, male?"

"No, baby," he replied, leading around the side of the house and toward the swampy woods. "My first promise."

***

Max didn't know where she'd taken him, and didn't care. They were alone, he could scent it. And that was all that mattered. He just wanted to be with her.

Share what he believed to be his newfound talents.

From the moment he'd stepped out of the car in the bayou, he'd felt a surge of power ripple through him. Not the kind he used in the ring, and not the kind he'd used in Benson's clinics during his torture sessions to keep himself from going mad. This was something else all together.

Something primal.

Something ancient.

He knew it in his bones.

He was what they were. Pantera. And his cat had awakened.

His gaze slid to the edge of the bayou. Elyon was standing there, her feet in just a few inches of water. As he watched, under the bright morning sky, she started to remove her clothing. Tight black pants. Gone. Jacket. Gone. Spandex top. Bye bye. Until she stood there completely naked.

Every inch of him hardened.

She was absolutely exquisite. A work of art. Long and lean, curvy ass, and a proper handful of breasts. And all his.

As he continued to stare, she turned to look him. Her blue eyes glistened and her short blond hair sparkled. And she smiled, welcomingly, hungrily.

"What are you waiting for, male?" she called out to him before diving beneath the slow moving current.

What was he waiting for? Nothing. Everything.

Eyes pinned to her shadow beneath the water, he started forward. But as he moved, a sudden dizzy sensation assaulted him. *What the hell?* He blinked, kept going. But the feeling only intensified. Hands fisted at his sides, mouth dry, it felt like his skin was melting, being pulled inward. He gritted his teeth and snarled a dark curse.

"Holy shit!" he heard Elyon call out.

But the sound was far away and slightly muffled. *What was happening?* His throat closed and for a blink of an eye it was like he was caught in a raging tornado. He couldn't see, couldn't hear. Couldn't breathe. His blood was boiling, churning.

And then…

It was over.

He was at the water's edge, his feet in the water…no. He looked down, his heart slamming against his ribs. No feet. Fur.

Paws.

Fuck.

He glanced up, found Elyon in the water. She was staring at him, eyes wide, lips curved into a beautiful smile.

"Max," she called. "You're gorgeous." She laughed. "I knew you would be. Black fur, amber eyes, white teeth. The water, it's on the border of the Wildlands. That's why you can shift."

He opened his mouth and tried to speak but only a growl escaped. He tried again, this time with his gaze pinned to Ely.

"Oh yeah," she said in return on another laugh. "Your mate's right here, baby."

He was his puma. How…?

Confused, but hungry for Elyon, he started toward her. But as soon as he was belly deep, the water repelled him. He snarled at it and backed up a foot.

"Just will it away, Max," she instructed gently. "As you walk toward me, force your male side forward. Your cat will listen. Especially now that you've released him. He wants you to mate with me. Just as my cat wants to mate with you."

His head filling with primal thoughts, Max did as she said. Forcing his cat back into the deeper water. And as the feline recoiled, the male pushed forward. Away. Out. Dizzy.

Skin.

Clothes.

Male.

Breathless, he looked around himself, chest deep in water.

"There it is," Elyon said, sounding proud and hungry and ready. "Don't worry, you'll have him back again soon. But for now, get over here. Your mate grows impatient."

A surge of animal heat remained inside of him and he growled at her. "We can't have that."

Pulling off his hoodie and shorts, leaving them to the bayou's slow current, he swam out to her. Instantly, he wrapped his arms around her and she in turn encircled his waist with her thighs.

For several seconds, they just clung to one another, gazing into each other's eyes, smiling like fools. Then Max asked, "So, what were you and your brother talking about when I walked up?"

"He's not my brother," she corrected. "But he is the only family I have."

Max shook his head slowly, brushing her nose with his. "Not true. You have me, baby."

She smiled and squeezed him tighter with her thighs. "You know what I mean."

"And you have Peter and Catherine Kudrow," he added with a soft kiss to her mouth. "If you want them."

She stilled.

Just as he'd expected her to.

"Ely…" he began.

She shook her head. "They're your parents."

"They want you, too."

"No…" Her voice broke.

"They do," he insisted, pulling her even tighter to him. He looked over her beautiful face, her wet eyelashes. "You are the daughter they never had. The one who not only rescued their son, but brought their family back together. You are their angel of life."

Her lips parted, but she didn't speak.

"They can't wait to get to know you, spoil you." He smiled broadly. "Mom even mentioned something about teaching you how to make the secret family cookie recipe."

Her eyes suddenly filled with tears and she turned away. She was touched, and it nearly killed him with happiness. The walls were coming down.

"Just think about it," he said gently. "We have all the time in the world now."

She nodded, turning back, wrapping her arms around his neck. "We have a lifetime, male. No matter what. It's you and me forever."

With a possessive growl, he leaned in and kissed her, hard and deep.

"After all, you've marked me," she whispered against his lips. "I'm yours, remember?"

His hands slipped beneath her and palmed her ass. "Oh, I remember."

"To do with as you will," she continued as the water lapped around them and sun heated their exposed skin. "For as long as you will."

"Baby…" he growled.

Her eyes closed and she purred. "Mark me again?"

He grinned, his body humming with a need he was just beginning to know. In time, he would learn who he was, what he was, as he put his old life behind him and embraced this new one with Elyon, his parents, and the Pantera.

One big happy family?

Ignoring the thread of worry that curled in his gut, he lifted his female up and set her down on his shaft. With a soft moan of appreciation, she settled in. Clinging to him, pressing her breasts against his chest, his tat, his wings. Reminding him, that no matter what happened, what was coming his way, she was his. She would be by his side, above him, and beneath him.

His love.

His mate.

His angel.

CHAPTER 10

The sky was taking on twilight as Raphael waited at the edge of the Wildlands for the young Healer to step into view. When she did, he moved like lightning, coming to stand in front of her in seconds, not at all surprised when she jumped back in alarm. Even for a Pantera he could move with uncanny silence. When he used it to play hide and seek with his daughter, she found it hilariously funny.

"Well?" he demanded.

The female heaved a faint sigh, her wide golden eyes troubled as she pushed back the silky red hair that had come loose from her ponytail.

"It's the same as it was with Hallie," she said.

Raphael scowled. "What does that mean?"

She gave a lift of her hands. "He's a human who was given Pantera blood. And for the most part he seems healthy."

Raphael latched onto the pertinent words. "For the most part?" he repeated.

She considered for a long moment. "This is going to sound impossible. But it's like there's something inside him—and her—that's not human or Pantera."

A thread of deep unease moved through Raphael. "What else could it be?"

The Healer shook her head. "I truly don't know. We've had many humans who've been given our blood, but this is different. I've never seen anything like it before."

"Is he dangerous?"

"No," she swiftly replied. "Whatever it is, it's dormant. There's no activity to it."

Raphael wasn't satisfied with that answer. "And what if it stops being dormant?"

The Healer lifted her chin and fixed him with a grave stare. "Just make sure none of these assets sets foot in the Wildlands."

As Raphael stood there, warm sunshine above, a shiver of deadly premonition inched down his spine. What the hell were they in for now?

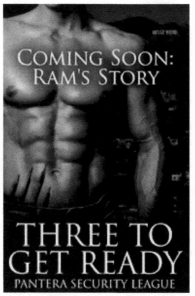

Coming soon the next book in the Pantera Security League series, THREE TO GET READY.

Enjoy a Sneak Peak of Alexandra's Ivy's newest suspense novel, KILL WITHOUT SHAME (Release Date: December 27)

KILL WITHOUT SHAME
(ARES SECURITY)
BY ALEXANDRA IVY

CHAPTER ONE

The Saloon was the sort of bar that catered to the locals in the quiet Houston neighborhood.

It was small, with lots of wood and polished brass. Overhead there was an open beam ceiling, with muted lights that provided a cozy atmosphere, and on the weekends they invited a jazz band to play quietly on the narrow stage.

Lucas spent most Friday evenings at the table tucked in a back corner. It was unofficially reserved for the five men who ran ARES Security.

The men liked the peaceful ambiance, the communal agreement that everyone should mind their own business, and the fact that the table was situated so no one could sneak up from behind.

Trained soldiers didn't want surprises.

At the moment, the bar was nearly empty. Not only was it a gray, wet Wednesday evening, but it was the first week of December. That meant Christmas madness was in full swing.

Perfectly normal people were now in crazy-mode as they scurried from store to store, battling one another for the latest, have-to-have gift. It was like Thunderdome without Tina Turner.

Currently Lucas and Teagan shared the bar with a young couple seated near the bay window at the front of the bar. Those two were oblivious to everything but each other. And closer to the empty stage was a table of college girls. Already at the giggly stage of drunk, they were all blatantly checking him out. At least when they weren't gawking at Teagan.

No biggie.

Both men were accustomed to female attention.

Teagan was a large, heavily muscled man with dark caramel skin, and golden eyes that he'd inherited from his Polynesian mother. He kept his hair shaved close to his skull, and as usual was dressed in a pair of camo pants and shit-kickers. He had an aggressive vibe that was only emphasized by the tight T-shirt that left his arms bare to reveal the numerous tattoos.

Lucas St. Clair, on the other hand, was wearing a thousand-dollar suit that was tailored to perfectly fit his lean body. His glossy black hair was smoothed away from his chiseled face that he'd been told could easily grace the covers of fashion magazines. As if he gave a shit.

His eyes were so dark they looked black. It wasn't until he was in the sunlight that it became obvious they were a deep, indigo blue.

Most assumed he was the less dangerous of the two men.

They'd be wrong.

But while the girls became increasingly more obvious in their attempts to attract their attention, neither man glanced in their direction.

Teagan because he already had a flock of women who included supermodels and two famous actresses.

And Lucas because… He grimaced.

To be honest, he wasn't sure why. He only knew that his interest in women hadn't been the same since he'd crawled out of that hellhole in Afghanistan. Not unless he counted the hours he spent brooding on one woman in particular.

The one who got away.

Lucas gave a sharp shake of his head, reaching for his shot of tequila. It slid down his throat like liquid fire, burning away the past.

Nothing like a twelve-year-old vintage to ease the pain.

Lucas glanced toward his companion's empty glass.

"Another round?" he asked.

"Sure." Teagan waited for Lucas to nod toward the bartender, who was washing glasses, at the same time keeping a sharp eye on his few customers. "I assume you're picking up the tab?"

Lucas cocked a brow. "Why do I always have to pick up the tab?"

"You're the one with the trust fund, amigo, not me," Teagan said with a shrug. "The only thing my father ever gave me was a concussion and an intimate knowledge of the Texas penal system."

Lucas snorted. It was common knowledge that Lucas would beg in the streets before he would touch a penny of the St. Clair fortune. Just as they all knew that Teagan had risen above his abusive background, and temporary housing in the penitentiary, to become a successful businessman. The younger man not only joined ARES, but he owned a mechanic shop that catered to a high-end clientele who had more money than sense when it came to their precious sports cars.

"I might break out the violins if I didn't know you're making a fortune," Lucas told his friend as the bartender arrived to replace their drinks with a silent efficiency.

"Hardly a fortune." Teagan downed a shot of tequila before he reached for his beer, heaving a faux sigh. "I have overhead out the ass, not to mention paying my cousins twice what they're worth. A word of warning, amigo. Never go into business with your family."

"Too late," Lucas murmured.

As far as he was concerned, the men who crawled out of that Taliban cave with him were his brothers. And the only family that mattered.

"True that." Teagan gave a slow nod, holding up his frosty glass. "To ARES."

Lucas clinked his glass against Teagan's in appreciation of the bond they'd formed.

"To ARES."

Drinking the tequila in one swallow, Lucas set aside his empty glass. There was a brief silence before Teagan at last spoke the words that'd no doubt been on the tip of his tongue since they walked through the door of the bar.

"Are you ever going to get to the point of why you asked to meet me here?" his friend bluntly demanded.

Lucas leaned back in his chair, arching his brows.

"Couldn't it just be because I enjoy your sparkling personality?"

Teagan snorted. "If I'd known this was a date I would have worn my lucky shirt."

"You need a shirt to get lucky?"

"Not usually." Teagan flashed his friend a mocking smile. "But I've heard you like to play hard to get."

Lucas grimaced at the direct hit. Yeah. Hard to get was one way to put it.

"I want to discuss Hauk," he admitted, not at all eager to think about his lack of a sex life.

About The Authors

Alexandra Ivy is a *New York Times* and *USA Today* bestselling author of the Guardians of Eternity, as well as the Sentinels, Dragons of Eternity and ARES series. After majoring in theatre she decided she prefers to bring her characters to life on paper rather than stage. She lives in Missouri with her family. Visit her website at alexandraivy.com.

New York Times and USA Today Bestselling Author, **Laura Wright** is passionate about romantic fiction. Though she has spent most of her life immersed in acting, singing and competitive ballroom dancing, when she found the world of writing and books and endless cups of coffee she knew she was home. Laura is the author of the bestselling Mark of the Vampire series and the USA Today bestselling series, Bayou Heat, which she co-authors with Alexandra Ivy.

Laura lives in Los Angeles with her husband, two young children and three loveable dogs.

CPSIA information can be obtained
at www.ICGtesting.com
Printed in the USA
LVHW050725050723
751553LV00015B/182